mary-kate

TWO

of a kind™

Island Girls

Surf, Sand and Secrets

Closer Than Ever

*Three great stories
in one big book!*

Look for more

titles:

mary-kateandashley
TWO of a Kind

Island Girls
by Nancy Butcher

Surf, Sand and Secrets
by Nancy Butcher

Closer Than Ever
by Judy Katschke

from the series created by
Robert Griffard & Howard Adler

HarperCollins*Entertainment*
An Imprint of HarperCollins*Publishers*

A PARACHUTE PRESS BOOK

A PARACHUTE PRESS BOOK
Parachute Publishing, L.L.C.
156 Fifth Avenue
Suite 325
NEW YORK
NY 10010

First published in the USA by HarperEntertainment 2001
Island Girls first published in Great Britain by HarperCollins*Entertainment* 2003
Surf, Sand and Secrets first published in Great Britain by HarperCollins*Entertainment* 2004
Closer Than Ever first published in Great Britain by HarperCollins*Entertainment* 2004

First published in this three-in-one edition by HarperCollins*Entertainment* 2005
HarperCollins*Entertainment* is an imprint of HarperCollins*Publishers* Ltd,
77-85 Fulham Palace Road, Hammersmith, London W6 8JB

TWO OF A KIND characters, names and all related indicia are trademarks of
Warner Bros.™ & © 2000.
TWO OF A KIND books created and produced by
Parachute Publishing, L.C.C. in cooperation with Dualstar Productions,
a division of Dualstar Entertainment Group, Inc.

Cover photograph courtesy of Dualstar Entertainment Group, Inc. © 2002

The HarperCollins *Children's Books* website address is
www.harpercollinschildrensbooks.co.uk

1

The authors assert the moral right to be
identified as the authors of these works.

ISBN 0 00 79092 1

Printed and bound in Great Britain by Clays Ltd, St Ives plc

mary-kateandashley

TWO of a kind™

Diaries

Island Girls

by Nancy Butcher

HarperCollins*Entertainment*
An Imprint of HarperCollins*Publishers*

A PARACHUTE PRESS BOOK

Chapter 1

Saturday

Dear Diary,

Aloha! That's how you say hello in Hawaiian. In a few minutes our plane will be landing at the airport in Hilo, Hawaii!

It's the first week of summer vacation and I'm on a school trip with some of my classmates from the White Oak Academy for Girls. White Oak is the boarding school in New Hampshire that I go to with my twin sister, Ashley. We're First Formers there (that means seventh-graders).

I can see long beaches and tall palm trees from the window of the plane. They're totally different from the green hills of New Hampshire. This trip is going to be awesome. Lots of my friends are here!

First there's Ashley's roommate, Phoebe Cahill, and my roommate and best bud, Campbell Smith (who's sitting next to me). There's also Julia Langstrom, Summer Sorenson and Elise Van Hook.

Dana Woletsky is here, too. I kind of wish she *wasn't* here. She's a superpopular First Former and she's never been nice to Ashley or me. I hope I won't have to spend time with her on this trip!

Our group isn't just all girls. The Harrington School for Boys is down the road from White Oak, and they sent some of the guys to Hawaii, too! Grant Marino, Hans Jensen, Seth Samuels and Devon Benjamin all came along. And I can't forget my cousin-dearest, Jeremy. He is so annoying! Diary, the only thing Ashley and I have in common with Jeremy is a last name.

"Hey, Mary-Kate," Jeremy said, walking up the aisle. "Hold this for a second, will you?"

I held out my hand. "Eeek!" I shrieked when he dropped something wiggly in my palm. Then I realised it was only a rubber spider.

Jeremy slapped his leg. "Ha! Gets 'em every time."

I threw the spider back at Jeremy. I hope he doesn't play practical jokes the whole time we're here. This trip is going to be a real challenge and practical jokes are the last thing we need!

We're going to Hawaii for four whole weeks. For the first half of our vacation we're participating in Wild Hawaii – a once-in-a-lifetime wilderness adventure, where we live off the land for twelve whole days. Imagine it, Diary – gathering food, building shelter, surviving on our own! Wow, it sounds even cooler now than when Ashley read me the description from the brochure!

For the second half of our vacation, we're off to an island resort, where our only responsibilities will be to relax and have fun!

Campbell elbowed me. "Did you know that certain kinds of flowers are edible?" she said. She was reading from a book called *The Outdoor Survival Guide.* Before we left for vacation, Campbell and I  had gone to the school library to take out books on camping in Hawaii. We wanted to make sure we were ready for anything!

I shook my head. "Nope. What else have you learned?"

Campbell jabbed her finger at another page. "That you can use the leaves of the aloe plant to treat minor burns and cuts."

I took a sip of the pineapple juice that the flight attendant had passed out. "Excellent! We'll totally be able to use all that information. Can I look through the books tonight?"

Campbell grinned. "Sure. After we finish reading these, we'll be experts at living in the wild."

It's a little scary to think that we'll be living the way people did zillions of years ago, without electricity and Ben and Jerry's ice cream. (Just kidding about the ice cream, Diary.) But we'll have a Wild Hawaii guide to tell us what to do and to take us to cool places on the island. I can't wait!

"Ms. Clare, will there be someone to carry our suitcases at the airport?" Summer asked from across the aisle.

Ms. Clare is the assistant headmistress of White Oak. She's really nice. Mr. Turnbull, the assistant

headmaster of Harrington, is here, too. When we first met him, he was really mean and scary – but these days he's much more laid-back. Right now he's sitting a few rows in front of me trying to play the ukulele!

"Why do you ask?" Ms. Clare replied.

Summer flipped her long blonde hair over her shoulders. "Because I brought, like, five or six suitcases."

Elise gasped. "Summer, Ms. Clare told us to pack *light*!"

Summer shrugged. "I thought I *was* packing light. Five suitcases isn't a lot of clothing."

Dana leaned across Summer and flashed me a smile. "Speaking of clothing, that is such a cute sundress, Mary-Kate!"

"Um, thanks," I said slowly. *Dana giving me a compliment? Unbelievable*, I thought.

"It really hides those extra pounds," she added.

I took a deep breath and counted to ten. I didn't want to say anything that would get me in trouble.

"Mary-Kate! Smile and say something for the camera!"

I glanced up. Phoebe's head popped over the seat in front of me. She was holding a video camera. I could tell by the blinking red light near the lens that she was recording.

"Hey, everyone!" I said with a big wave. "Wish you were here!"

Phoebe has the coolest job on this vacation. She will be camping on the beach with us, but she's not part of the Wild Hawaii challenge. She's here to capture all the action on video. The footage will be shown at a special school assembly this autumn. (I hope she doesn't catch me doing anything stupid!)

"Attention, passengers," the pilot announced over the loudspeaker. "Please fasten your seat belts."

Yay! We're almost ready to land. Hello, Hilo!

Two of a Kind Diaries

Dear Diary,

I am now officially a wilderness girl. And I have to tell you, it's not that bad!

Last night we stayed at the hotel. This morning Mr. Turnbull and Ms. Clare took us to the camp, which is about a mile away. They'll be with us only part of the time at Wild Hawaii. The rest of the time they'll stay at the hotel.

The camp is a big open area on the beach surrounded by palm trees. To our left is the ocean. To our right are a bunch of twisty trails lined with exotic plants and flowers.

Our guide's name is Maleko. That's how you say Mark in Hawaiian. (Maleko told me that my name in Hawaiian is Mai Ke!)

Maleko has long black hair that he wears back in a ponytail, and he has huge muscles. He must exercise ten hours a day or something. Maleko was dressed in denim cutoffs and a T-shirt that said NO FEAR. He wasn't wearing shoes.

"Wild Hawaii is not your typical vacation," were the first words out of Maleko's mouth. "Wild

Hawaii is an experience that will challenge you physically, mentally and emotionally."

"That doesn't sound like a vacation at all," Jeremy said.

"For the next twelve days you will be in survival mode," Maleko went on. "That means you will have limited supplies. Only a few articles of clothing and some camping gear."

"So much for Summer's five suitcases," Mary-Kate whispered to me.

Elise's brown eyes grew really wide. "Can we bring makeup?" she asked.

"No way." Maleko folded his arms across his chest.

"Not even *lip gloss*?" I asked. "Lip gloss is a big part of my life!"

"Not even lip gloss," Maleko replied.

"But this is a survival trip," Summer cut in. "How am I supposed to survive without makeup?"

Phoebe whipped her camera around, pointing it right at Summer. "Raw emotion! Good! Summer, please tell us how you feel about having to live without makeup for twelve days."

Summer's expression changed as soon as she saw the video camera. She plastered a big smile on her face. "I said, this is going to be a blast!" she exclaimed.

I giggled. Phoebe wrinkled her nose.

"Each of you will be given a job to do," Maleko continued, "like pitching tents and collecting food. Everyone must work as a team to survive. If you are not a team player or you don't complete your job for the day, you will be eliminated from the Wild Hawaii challenge and sent back to the hotel."

"That's a harsh rule," Seth commented.

"It didn't say that in the brochure," Dana added.

"When do we get to have fun?" I asked.

Maleko smiled. "The fun comes from knowing that you can survive in the wild. It's going to be tough at first, but at the end of the twelve days, you'll find out how strong you really are."

Maleko's words were starting to pump me up. I could tell everyone else was getting into the idea, too.

"You will see things on this island that you've never seen before," Maleko went on, "and you'll find a part of yourself that you never knew existed." He looked around at all of us. "Are you guys up for the challenge?"

"Yeah!" we all cried together.

"Good." Maleko nodded. "I haven't even told you the best part yet. Because teamwork is so important in Wild Hawaii, at the end of the twelve days the person who I think has demonstrated the best teamwork will win a special prize."

Teamwork is my middle name, I thought. *And I am always up for a challenge – especially if it means winning something!* "What is the prize?" I asked.

"A one-hundred-dollar shopping spree in Hawaii," Maleko said.

Everyone started talking excitedly. "That prize is mine!" Hans announced.

"No way, dude," Grant told him. "*I'm* going to win."

I tapped Phoebe on the shoulder. She turned her video camera on me. "Yes?"

"You can get *this* on tape," I exclaimed. "The only person who is going to win that shopping spree is *me*!"

Chapter 2

Sunday

Dear Diary,

Ever since Maleko mentioned the hundred-dollar prize, everyone has been going out of their way to show that they are a team player. Hans offered to carry my backpack. Julia gave a few people some of her muffin from breakfast. Even Jeremy got in on the act and told jokes to keep up the group's spirits.

"Mary-Kate." Campbell joined me as I checked out the beach. "Don't you think we should tell the other kids what we learned from our survival guides?"

"Sure. That's what good team players would do," I agreed. I sat down on the sand. Nearby, a patch of orange orchids waved in the breeze.

I turned to Campbell as she sat next to me. "What would you buy if you won the hundred dollars?" I asked her.

Campbell grinned. "I would definitely hit the sports store at the hotel," she said.

"Me, too," I agreed. Campbell and I have a lot of things in common. That's one reason why we are such good friends.

"All right, people, gather around!" Maleko

waved to everyone and I saw the muscles ripple in his arm. Diary, that guy must *live* at the gym.

Campbell and I headed over to the group. We all sat down in a circle. Maleko held up his clipboard.

"I've divided you all into teams of two and three for each job," he explained.

Maleko slowly read off our names and jobs. Finally, he got to me. "Mary-Kate, you have fishing duty," he said. "Each day you have to catch the group's dinner. Campbell will be your partner."

Campbell and I high-fived. Fishing with my best friend. This was going to be great!

Of course, I'd been fishing only once in my life and that was when I was five. But how hard could it be?

Maleko said we had to make our own fishing poles. Normally, I would have panicked at the news. But Campbell and I read all about how to do it in one of our camping books!

"First, we should find some bamboo," Campbell suggested.

This took longer than we thought it would. But only because we stopped to help Julia carry some heavy pieces of wood. She was on firewood duty.

Once we found some long, skinny pieces of bamboo, we needed to find fishing line and hooks.

"Do you think Maleko brought us some?" I asked hopefully.

Campbell shook her head. "No way," she said. "But I bet someone has some dental floss. That might work as fishing line."

"What an excellent idea!" I said. "And we can borrow some paper clips from Phoebe to use as hooks. She always has some in her backpack."

"Mary-Kate, we are brilliant!" Campbell cheered.

When we were done making the fishing rods, we decided to use some sharp rocks to carve our initials into the bamboo. That way, we would be able to tell them apart. I felt really proud of myself, Diary! I was starting to feel at one with nature already.

 On a less exciting note, we needed bait, so we had to pull slimy little worms out of the sand and put them in a small bucket. All I can really say about that is – yuck! We used some really big shells to dig with.

"So far so good," Campbell said when our bucket was full.

"Yeah, but now we actually have to *catch* the fish," I pointed out.

Campbell plonked down our bucket of bait and fishing poles into the wooden boat that Maleko had given us. "Don't worry, we can do it."

We put on our life jackets and climbed into the boat. Then we each took an oar. We paddled out to a small lagoon. I noticed Summer and Jeremy rustling through the bushes in the distance, picking berries. Summer didn't look too happy about it. I guess she wasn't as excited about the wilderness as I was.

The water was so clear all around us I could see schools of tiny yellow fish swimming near the surface.

"I am *not* eating those guys," I told Campbell, pointing at the fish. "They are way too cute!"

"Don't worry," Campbell said. "That's not what we're fishing for. They're too small."

We fished for about two hours. By the time we rowed back to shore we had caught ten big fish!

Campbell and I delivered the fish to Dana, Elise and Seth. They were the cooking crew.

"Excellent!" Seth exclaimed. "We'll fry these babies up for dinner."

Thanks to some tips from our books, we helped the cooking crew get the fire started in no time at all. We even showed them how to clean the fish!

"You guys are really the best," Elise said. "I definitely did not want to clean those fish myself."

We helped out a lot today, Diary. Maybe Campbell or I will even win the prize! But since we did everything together, I decided that if I won the prize, I would share it with Campbell.

"I was just thinking the same thing, MK!" she said when I told her.

Campbell and I are an awesome team.

Dear Diary,

Maleko put me, Hans and Devon in charge of pitching tents for the whole group. (Maleko, aka Mr. Extreme, told us he never uses a tent. He would rather sleep in the open.)

"Have you guys ever been camping before?" I asked Hans and Devon.

"I've been camping with my family a few times," Devon replied. "But my parents usually put the tents together."

Hans shook his head. "I've never been camping before," he said. "How about you, Ashley?"

"I was in the Bluebird Scout Troop for five years and we went camping every year," I said. "We're in luck. I'm a total *expert* at building tents."

"Excellent!" Hans said. "Then what should we do first?"

"That's easy," Devon said. "We put the poles together."

"Right," I agreed. "They make up the framework for the tent."

We each grabbed some poles and examined them. "What do these little red dots at the end of each pole mean?" Hans asked.

"I bet we're supposed to match them up to each other," Devon guessed.

I shook my head. "I've seen tents like this before," I explained. "I think this brand is just made with red dots at the end. We have to figure out ourselves which poles match up."

Devon shrugged. "Are you sure?" he asked doubtfully.

"Pretty sure," I replied.

"Then let's get started," Hans said. He reached for a few poles.

"Let me hold that up for you." I steadied a pole so Hans could attach it to another one.

"Thanks, Ashley," Hans said.

I smiled. Was this teamwork or what?

A few minutes later I snapped together the last two poles. I stood between Devon and Hans as we all examined our work. "Looks good to me!" I said.

"I guess so," Devon said. He didn't look one hundred percent convinced. I knew he was still thinking about the dots. But he'd realise I was right once we were done.

"What's next?" Hans asked.

"Now we attach the tents to the poles," I said.

Devon picked up one of the tarps and threw it over the pole. But I knew from camping that you had to carefully attach certain pieces of the tent to each pole – not just throw it over.

"Devon, that's not how you do it," I said.

"Yes, it is," he insisted. "I definitely remember watching my parents do this part."

"It looks okay to me," Hans said, checking out the tarp.

"Guys, trust me," I replied. "I know what I'm talking about. Didn't I know how to put all the poles together?"

"But, Ashley—" Devon started.

"We have to focus on being a good team," I interrupted. "That means listening to one another."

Devon kicked a foot in the sand. "Fine. We'll do it your way."

"Thanks," I said. Once I showed the guys how to fasten the tents, it didn't take us long to finish them all.

"We're almost done!" I said excitedly. "All we have left is to put in the stakes."

"Even *I* know what to do with these," Hans said, picking up the bag of metal stakes. "We tie them to the tents and then pound them into the ground, right?"

"Well, sort of," I replied. "It's just the other way around. First you put the stakes into the ground and *then* you attach them to the tents."

"Are you sure, Ashley?" Devon asked. "That doesn't sound right to me. I think we should do it Hans's way."

"But I know I'm right about this," I replied. "That's how we used to do it at camp."

Devon scowled at me. Hans didn't look too happy either.

Maybe I should compromise, I thought. *That's what a good team player would do, right?* "Okay," I said. "Let's each do it our own way."

"Fine," Hans and Devon said together. We pounded the stakes in silence.

We finished just as the sun went down. I stood up and examined our work. A few of the tents were a little crooked – but they didn't look half bad!

"Congratulations, team," I said. "We did a great job."

Jeremy and Summer, who had been collecting berries, came over. "Hey, Ashley," Jeremy said, "I didn't know you had enough brain cells to build a tent!"

I frowned at Jeremy as he plopped himself into the nearest one.

The whole thing immediately collapsed. I gasped.

"Hey!" Jeremy cried out.

Summer climbed into another tent. That one fell down, too. I started to get a little worried.

"Ashley, since you're such a tent expert," Devon said, "maybe you can explain why all our tents are falling down."

"I'm sure it's just these two," I said, starting to put one tent back together.

Before I could fix it, Maleko came over and surveyed the damage. "What's going on?" he asked.

"We're having a problem with our job," Hans said slowly.

"What's the problem?" Maleko asked.

"Ashley made us do everything *her* way," Devon said, "and now our tents are falling down."

My mouth fell open. "It's not that I didn't listen," I said. "I just wanted to do things the *right* way."

Maleko kneeled down and inspected each tent. "You guys made a big mistake here," he said after a moment. "None of these tents will hold up. Didn't you know that the red dots on the end of the poles are supposed to match up with each other?"

Oops, I thought. *I guess I was wrong about that.* I could feel Hans and Devon staring at me.

"Does this mean we have to sleep at the hotel tonight?" Summer asked. She glanced at her sandals. "Because I could really use a pedicure!"

Maleko stood up and shook his head. "We're staying right here." He looked at Hans and Devon. "Okay. Let's take down these tents and start over. Otherwise we're all sleeping out in the open tonight."

I felt awful. Hans and Devon had been right. "I'm sorry," I said to Hans and Devon. "I should have listened to your ideas. I promise, this time, we'll build the tents however you want to do it."

"Wait a second, Ashley," Maleko said. "You don't have to rebuild the tents."

I was confused. "Why not?" I asked.

Maleko folded his arms. "You broke rule number one. You weren't a good team player. And I told you what happens if you break the rules."

I gulped. "But—" I started.

"Sorry, Ashley," Maleko said. "You're out of Wild Hawaii."

Chapter 3

Monday

Dear Diary,

Last night was the loneliest night of my life! I sat in the hotel all by myself wishing I was back at Wild Hawaii.

Ms. Clare and Mr. Turnbull had rooms on the same floor as me, but they don't really count as someone to hang out with.

This morning I wandered down to the pool to catch some rays. The hotel staff here are pretty cool. They are nice and friendly and will even bring you a smoothie if you ask. I might enjoy it here if I wasn't feeling so bad for getting kicked out of the game!

"Hi, Ashley," Ms. Clare said, sitting down on the lounge chair next to mine. She was decked out in vacation gear – a tennis dress, a white floppy hat and sneakers. "Are you having a nice day?"

I shook my head sadly. "Not really," I said. "I can't believe I'm not going back to Wild Hawaii."

Ms. Clare patted me on the arm. "Don't worry," she said. "You and I can explore lots of interesting places. We'll go anywhere you want to visit."

I smiled. "Thanks," I replied. "That sounds great." But inside I was still sad. I liked Ms. Clare and all, but I wanted to spend my vacation with my friends!

Ms. Clare seemed to read my mind. "Don't forget, Ashley," she went on, "if *you* were sent back to the hotel, there *is* a chance that other students will get sent back, too. Then we can all have fun together!"

My smile got a little brighter. Ms. Clare was right. I might have a friend to hang out with sooner or later. I just hoped it was *sooner*!

Dear Diary,

I'm so bummed out about Ashley not being in the game any more. I can't believe she was kicked out! I hope she's not too miserable back at the hotel.

This is our second night at camp. Last night everyone feasted on the fish that Campbell and I caught.

I have to say, Diary, it was the best fish I had ever tasted! There's just something about eating food you catch yourself, you know?

After dinner, we all helped clean up. Then we sat around the campfire while Maleko pointed out the constellations. It seemed like there were a million stars in the sky. Is it my imagination, or does the sky

 seem a lot bigger when you're camping out on a beach in Hawaii?

This morning we were all awake at the crack of dawn. I could have slept a lot longer, but Maleko was already up yelling, "Okay, people, let's go, let's go, LET'S GO!"

I staggered out of my tent and down to the beach. I washed my face with a little bowl of cold water. Fresh water is hard to come by. We collect only a certain amount from a freshwater spring each day. Just between you and me, Diary, I really miss indoor plumbing!

Phoebe snuck up on me and tried to videotape me just as I started brushing my teeth.

"Go away!" I yelled at her, although it sounded like "Ro raway!" since my toothbrush was hanging out of my mouth.

Then it was time to start our jobs for the day. I met Campbell down at our boat.

"I have an idea that will help us catch more fish," Campbell said. "I read about it in one of our books. Instead of using worms for bait, we can use little fish. We might be able to catch more big fish that way."

"Excellent thinking," I said. "I read that big fish really like to eat minnows."

"Those are the little silver ones, right?" Campbell asked.

I nodded. "Minnows hang out in shallow pools of water. We can scoop them up in buckets."

"Mary-Kate, I am so glad you're my partner," Campbell said.

Diary, I'm so glad Campbell is my partner, too! Her idea worked really well. We caught twice as many fish as yesterday. I can't believe it – just a few days ago, my idea of fishing was ordering the fried seafood special in the dining hall!

Campbell and I got a round of applause at dinner for bringing back so much food. Even Dana complimented us. I was really surprised. She never gives out compliments – unless she's talking about herself!

"We're having berries and coconuts for dessert," Summer said, as everyone finished eating. "Jeremy collected the coconuts."

Grant turned to Jeremy. "Bring them on!" he said.

Jeremy tapped a finger against his lip. "Coconuts . . . now where did I put the coconuts?"

Summer glared at him. "Jeremy! You *did* collect the coconuts, right?"

"Of course I did," Jeremy said, folding his arms. "But then they kind of . . . disappeared."

"How did that happen?" Maleko asked.

Jeremy shrugged. "I think it happened right around the time when I . . . ate them."

I gasped. "Jeremy, how could you?" I asked. Then I remembered that if there is one thing in life Jeremy can't resist, it's food!

Maleko was *not* happy. "Jeremy, you and I need to have a little talk," he said, standing up.

Jeremy followed Maleko into his tent. A few minutes later Maleko joined the group again – but Jeremy didn't.

"Okay, troops," Maleko said. "I have a surprise for you. Tomorrow we're going on a special hike."

I perked up. "Where are you taking us?" I asked.

Maleko smiled. "It's a secret. But I promise, it will be like nothing you've ever seen before!"

Everyone started buzzing excitedly. Where could we be going?

Dear Diary,

My wish has come true! Ms. Clare just told me that someone else got kicked out of Wild Hawaii. She wasn't sure who it was, though.

But it doesn't matter as long as I have company! I can't wait. We can hang out at the pool together and go to the beach . . .

Someone knocked loudly on my door. I jumped off the bed and rushed over to answer it.

Who would it be? Mary-Kate? Julia? Seth? Grant?

I grabbed the handle and pulled open the door.

"Yo, Ashley. Got any food?" My cousin pushed past me into the room. I stared at him open-mouthed as he flopped onto my bed and grabbed the remote control.

Let's back up a second. Did I say it *didn't* matter who it was?

Well, I was wrong!

Of all people, why, oh, why, did I have to get stuck with Jeremy?

Chapter 4

Tuesday

Dear Diary,

Maleko kept us in suspense the whole morning.

"Are we going to see a waterfall?" Devon asked.

"Are we going to pick flowers?" Elise guessed.

"Are we going to a restaurant?" Summer chimed in. I think she is really starting to miss the hotel!

Maleko spread out his arms and grinned. "Way better than that. We're going to visit a volcano!"

Campbell and I jumped up and down. This was going to be so exciting!

"The name of the volcano is Kilauea," Maleko said as we began our hike. "It has several craters attached to it that are made from cooled lava."

"Excellent!" Hans said.

"The crater we're going to is called Pu'u Huluhulu," Maleko went on.

I laughed. "Try saying that three times fast."

Phoebe videotaped us marching down a narrow, muddy trail that led us to Pu'u Huluhulu. Along the way, we saw all sorts of plants with weird names like *akala* and *iliau*.

It took us an hour or so to get to the volcano. (It was so far away that we cheated a little and took a bus part of the way.) But once we were there, I couldn't believe my eyes! The ground was hard and black from lava that had dried up years ago.

"Take a look at this," Maleko said, stepping up to the edge of the crater. We followed behind him.

"Wow!" I cried. Right in front of us was a real live volcano! I could see small patches of red-yellow lava coming out of it.

"Can we hike over there?" Grant asked, taking a step forward.

Maleko put a hand on Grant's shoulder and pulled him back. "I don't think so," he said. "That lava is over two thousand degrees. You don't want to get much closer than this. But there are lots of other things we can see from right here."

"What is this?" Dana asked, pointing to a big black thing that looked like a sculpture sticking out of the ground.

"That's a lava tree," Maleko explained. "Years ago, when hot lava flowed past here, it made a cast around the tree and dried.

In fact, there are lava trees all over the area."

"What about those craters over there?" Seth asked, pointing to a few deep holes that surrounded the volcano. "What are they called?"

Maleko looked out across the cavern. "Well, that one to the left is called Halema'uma'u," he said. "It's very special because the natives believe that the ancient fire goddess, Pele, lives inside."

Campbell wrinkled her nose. "Ancient fire goddess?" she repeated.

Maleko waved us into a tighter circle. "Pele is a very powerful goddess," he said. "Legend says that when she gets angry, she makes the volcano erupt."

"Has anyone ever seen her?" Hans asked.

"Some people say they have," Maleko said. "But no one knows for sure if she exists."

Come on, I thought. It was a cool story and all, but I didn't believe in fire goddesses.

Maleko talked a little more about the history of the area. Phoebe stood up with her camera and began taping the landscape. Soon Maleko decided it was time to head back to camp.

"Hey, Mary-Kate," Campbell said. "Why don't we take a souvenir?" She held up a piece of volcanic rock.

"Why didn't I think of that?" I said. I picked up my own piece of rock and took an extra one for Ashley. I knew it wasn't the same as being on the hike with us, but I thought it might cheer her up a little.

When we returned to camp, Campbell and I sat under a palm tree and checked out our souvenirs.

Maleko walked over to us. "What have you got there?" he asked.

"We took some of the volcano home with us," Campbell explained. "Cool, right?"

Maleko's eyes widened. "Oh, no," he said.

"Oh, no, what?" I asked.

Maleko sat down next to us under the tree. "I can't believe I didn't tell you the most important part of the legend of Pele," he said.

Campbell and I glanced at each other. "What is it?" she asked.

"Well, the legend says that if you take a piece of Pele's volcano, you must leave a gift in exchange," Maleko explained. "Otherwise you will be cursed. You will have horrible luck – forever!"

I breathed a sigh of relief. I thought he was going to tell us something serious! "You don't really believe that stuff, do you?" I asked.

"Yeah, those legends are just superstition," Campbell added. "It said so in my guidebook."

Maleko shrugged. "Many people have experienced the anger of Pele when they took something of hers and didn't leave a gift behind," he said.

Maleko seemed so serious, I almost laughed. "Well . . . thanks for the warning," I said. But I agreed with Campbell. There is no such thing as an ancient curse.

Dear Diary,

Auuuuggghhhhh! I thought getting kicked out of Wild Hawaii was bad. But being stuck at the hotel with Jeremy is much, much worse.

This morning he ate my breakfast right off my plate. Then he took my postcards. But the worst was when I was sitting by the pool, catching some rays. "Hey, Ashley, check it out!"

I glanced up from my magazine. Jeremy was standing on the diving board, waving like mad. He was wearing a green bathing suit with yellow smiley faces all over it.

"Cowabunga!" Jeremy shouted. He jumped off the diving board and curled himself into a ball.

Splash! A huge wave sprayed all over me.

Jeremy surfaced and pointed at me. "Good one, huh?" He laughed. "And that wasn't even my biggest wave!"

I looked around for Ms. Clare to see if she was watching. But she was on the tennis courts nearby playing doubles with some people from Boise, Idaho, that she had met at breakfast. She kept hitting the ball out of the court and cracking up.

Time to leave, I thought. I grabbed my sarong and my soaking-wet magazine and made a run for it.

I missed everyone at Wild Hawaii so much. What were they doing? Were they having fun? Did they miss me as much as I missed them?

I decided to sneak over there and find out. I bought a double strawberry ice cream cone at the hotel café for the trip. Then I headed outside and started down the trail that led to the camp.

I hid behind some bushes as I got closer to camp. I didn't want to run into Maleko. I was still feeling a little embarrassed that I was the first one kicked out of Wild Hawaii.

I could see the tops of the tents through the bushes. Then I heard voices. It was Summer and Elise! They were walking towards me.

"Did you notice all that seaweed just lying around on the beach?" Summer said. "We could collect it and wrap ourselves up in it."

"Why would we want to wrap ourselves in all that slime?" Elise asked.

"My mom gets seaweed wraps at a spa and they are really expensive," Summer explained. "But we would be getting one for free!"

I stepped out from behind a tree. "Hey, guys," I whispered.

"Ashley!" Summer and Elise ran over and gave me big hugs.

"What are you doing here?" Elise asked.

"I just wanted to visit," I replied. "Is Maleko around?"

"No. Everyone else went swimming," Summer said. "They're all down by the beach."

Elise's eyes grew big. "Wow, an ice cream cone."

Summer licked her lips. "It looks so delicious."

"Want some?" I offered, holding out the cone.

"Sure!" Summer and Elise said at the same time. Diary, I don't think I have ever seen two people eat ice cream so fast!

"It must be nice on the outside." Elise's shoulders slumped.

"It's okay," I replied, shrugging. I told them all about the pool and the smoothies and the TV with one hundred and twenty channels.

"I wish I was back at the hotel with you, Ashley," Summer said wistfully.

"Me, too!" Elise agreed. "This roughing-it thing is cool – but sipping smoothies by the pool sounds much cooler!"

"You're lucky you got kicked out," Summer added.

"Hey, wait a minute," I said. "I have a great idea."

"No, *I* have a great idea," Elise replied.

Summer smiled. "No, I do! If Ashley had no trouble getting kicked out, then *we* shouldn't have a problem either! Right, Elise?"

"Right!" Elise said.

"Cool!" I cried. "And I know just how you can do it."

Chapter 5

Wednesday

Dear Diary,

I have a really good feeling about today.

I'm not sure why. Maybe it's because

Campbell and I keep helping out so many people with advice from our survival guide. Last night we showed Summer a new plant that grows the best-tasting fruit. We helped Grant dry firewood in record time and figured out a cool way to make our tents extra cosy. Diary, we are becoming real wilderness girls!

Campbell and I skipped down to the beach that afternoon to go fishing. As we approached the water, Campbell stopped in her tracks. "Oh, no!"

"What is it?" I asked.

And then I saw. Next to the boat our bucket of bait was lying on its side in the sand. There were no minnows left anywhere!

"How did this happen?" I cried.

Campbell groaned. "We can't collect more minnows now. The high tide probably washed all their pools away."

"Well, we still have to catch food for dinner," I

said. "So what do you think we should do?"

"Let's just dig up some worms and head out," Campbell replied.

"Okay," I agreed. "Go team!" I added, trying to keep our spirits up.

Campbell peeked inside the boat. "Um, Mary-Kate, where are our digging shells?"

I followed her gaze. "I don't know." I scratched my head. "I thought I left them right there."

Campbell sighed. "I guess we'll have to find new ones."

We spent the next ten minutes looking for big shells that were good for digging. But the only ones we could find were either broken or too small.

"Come on. We're wasting time," I said, handing Campbell a broken shell. "Let's just use these."

We dug and we dug. But for some reason, all the worms were in hiding today, because we found only ten. By the end of the day we had caught a grand total of five fish. If you want to get technical, five not very big fish.

As we trudged back to camp, the cooking crew saw us coming and cheered. "How many do you have for us today?" Dana called.

Campbell and I exchanged a glance. "Um, five," she mumbled.

"That's it?" Seth asked, looking inside our bucket.

I quickly made up an excuse. "There were bad fishing conditions today," I said. "It was, uh, too sunny."

"Too sunny?" Elise echoed.

"Yeah," I went on. "Our survival guide said that some fish don't like too much sun."

Okay, so our book never told us that. But I had to say something, Diary!

"This isn't enough food," Seth grumbled. "Everyone is going to be hungry."

I stared down at the sand. I didn't want anyone to be disappointed with us.

"Don't worry, guys," Dana said. "I know this recipe my mom and dad make a lot. If I mix some coconut and coconut juice in with the fish and make this stew-y stuff out of it, it will seem like a lot more food."

I couldn't believe that she was being so nice about the whole thing. Dana, of all people!

The stew turned out to be really delicious. But I had a hard time enjoying it. Right before dinner Campbell and I overheard some people talking about us.

"They were probably goofing off instead of

catching fish," Seth grumbled to Julia.

"Maybe they think because they caught a bunch of fish yesterday, they can slack off," Julia suggested.

"Do you think Maleko is going to send them back to the hotel, just like Ashley and Jeremy?" Hans asked.

I gasped. The situation wasn't that serious, was it?

"Don't worry," Campbell whispered to me. "We did really well yesterday and the day before. Tomorrow will be fine."

"You're probably right," I said, feeling a little better. "Anyone can have a bad day."

In fact, the group kind of forgot about the fish when Summer announced that there would be no berries for dessert.

"No dessert?" Hans cried. "Why not?"

"I gave myself a berry facial before dinner," Summer explained, "and before I knew it I used up all the berries. Sorry!"

She didn't seem too sorry, though. She wasn't even upset when Maleko told her that she had broken the rules and would have to leave.

You know what else, Diary? I might have been imagining it – but

I could swear I saw Summer give Elise a high five when she left to go back to the hotel. What's up with *that*?

Dear Diary,
    "Ashley, check out this top! And look at this! Have you ever seen such a beautiful sundress before?"
    Summer was speed-reading through a pile of teen magazines. You would think she hadn't seen a fashion magazine in years and years.
    We were lounging in the hotel hot tub. There was a full moon in the sky, the air was really warm, and the best part was, Jeremy wasn't around!
    "Why didn't I think of this before?" Summer asked, putting down a magazine. She picked up her smoothie and raised it in the air. "I owe my freedom to you, Ashley. Thanks for the berry facial idea!"
    I raised my smoothie, too. "And tomorrow night, if Elise does what she's supposed to do, she'll be free, too!"
    We clinked cups. Life was very, very good.

Chapter 6

Thursday

Dear Diary,

I never should have got up today, because everything went wrong! It all started after breakfast.

"Campbell," I said, as we all finished eating, "since the cooking crew covered for us yesterday, why don't we offer to clean up breakfast for them?"

"Sounds good to me," Campbell said.

"Can Campbell and I clean up for you?" I asked Seth, Dana and Elise. "You know, to thank you for helping us out with dinner yesterday."

"Sure!" Dana said.

"That would be awesome," Seth added.

"Yeah, thanks, you guys," Elise chimed in.

Dana, Elise and Seth walked off as Campbell and I started to throw paper plates into a garbage bag.

I nodded and waved to them. "This shouldn't take too long," I said to Campbell as I threw away a mango stone.

I was right. A few minutes later we had packed everything into the garbage bag.

"Make sure you tie the bag tightly," Campbell said. "It's pretty breezy."

"No problem," I said, and twisted the top of the bag into a knot.

"Finished!" Campbell exclaimed. "Time to go swimming!"

We had the best time swimming in the lagoon with some of the other kids. But when Campbell and I came back a few hours later—

"Oh, no!" I gasped. Garbage was scattered all over the sand. And our bag was wide open!

"Mary-Kate, I told you to tie the bag tightly," Campbell complained.

"I did!" I cried. "At least I thought I did."

Campbell sighed. "Well, we'd better clean up this trash before Maleko sees it."

But we were too late. Seth, Dana, Elise and Maleko walked up to us.

"What happened here?" Maleko asked, surveying the mess.

"We told the cooking crew we would clean up for them," I groaned. "But I guess we didn't tie the garbage bag good enough."

"We're really sorry," Campbell said.

"We'll clean it up right now," I added.

"I'll help," Dana offered. "Then we'll finish faster."

"That's the spirit!" Maleko said.

Seth and Elise slowly joined in. But I was pretty

sure they weren't happy that they had to do it.

"So much for being helpful," Campbell muttered as we started picking up the garbage again.

"No kidding," I said. "We'll definitely have to catch extra fish to make up for this one. Let's start early today."

"Sounds good to me," Campbell said.

Half an hour later we headed over to the boat.

"Boy, these past two days haven't been much fun," Campbell said.

"Tell me about it," I said. "First our bait and digging shells disappear. Then we mess up garbage duty."

"Campbell," I said slowly, "I know this is going to sound weird, but do you think all this bad luck we've been having has anything to do with the curse of Pele?"

"You mean if we don't leave her a gift we'll have bad luck forever?" Campbell snorted. "Give me a break, Mary-Kate. We just had a bad morning, that's all."

I took a deep breath. Campbell was probably right. I mean, I didn't believe in the legend before, so why should I believe it now? So what if we had a little bad luck. It was just a coincidence.

We climbed into the rowing boat. "Okay, let's

make a pact that all bad luck ends right now," I said.

"Agreed," Campbell said. She glanced around the inside of the boat. "Uh, MK? Did you do something with the oars?"

I shook my head. "No. Why?"

"Because they're not here," Campbell said.

I scanned the nearby beach. There was no sign of the oars there either. Where could they have gone? I looked out into the lagoon.

That's when I saw them. They were floating way out in the water. "Campbell, look!" I cried.

"How did they fall out of the rowing boat?" Campbell asked.

"I don't know, but we have to go after them," I replied. "Let's paddle ourselves out there with our hands."

"Isn't that going to be hard?" Campbell asked.

"We'll find out," I said as I started paddling.

"I feel like my arms are about to fall off," Campbell grumbled after a few minutes.

"Me, too," I panted. "But we can do it." I leaned over the side of the boat. "Paddle harder!"

Then I realised Campbell was leaning over the same side of the boat as I was.

"Maybe you should paddle on the other side," I pointed out. "We don't want to—"

Too late. The rowing boat tipped over and we fell right into the water.

I bobbed under the waves and then surfaced and spat out some salt water. Campbell popped up next to me.

"Oh, no!" She groaned. "Phoebe is taping us from the beach!"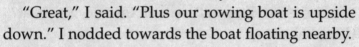

I looked over. Phoebe put down her camera and waved at us as she walked away.

"Great," I said. "Plus our rowing boat is upside down." I nodded towards the boat floating nearby.

I swam a few strokes closer to rescue it. "What's all this slimy brown stuff in the water?" I asked, swimming through it.

"Mary-Kate, it's our bait!" Campbell cried. "It's getting in your hair."

"Eeewwww!" I shrieked. I dived under the water and shook my head. Then I swam away as quickly as I could.

Campbell managed to flip the rowing boat and climb back in. I swam over and climbed in, too. Then we paddled slowly to shore and dragged ourselves onto the beach.

"I have a feeling we're not going to catch many

fish today." Campbell plopped down onto the sand.

"Tell me about it," I said, sitting next to her. "I'm really beginning to think Maleko was right. Maybe we *are* cursed!"

Campbell let some sand trickle through her fingers. "Mary-Kate, that's stupid," she said. "There is no way we're having all this bad luck just because we didn't leave Pele a gift."

But I didn't think it was stupid. This was just too much of a coincidence for me.

"Hey," Dana called. "Are you guys taking a break?" She was walking towards us, carrying a basket of berries.

"Hey, Dana," I mumbled.

Dana stopped and gave us a once-over. "Why are you all wet?" she asked.

"We fell out of the rowing boat," Campbell explained in a low voice. I braced myself for an insult.

"Want some berries?" Dana asked. "I'm making them into a soup for dinner tonight."

My eyebrows shot up. Was that all she was going to say?

"Uh, thanks," I replied. I took a handful and popped one in my mouth. It was delicious.

"So what's going on?" Dana asked, putting down her basket.

"We kind of had an accident," Campbell explained.

"What happened?" Dana asked, sounding concerned. "Are you okay?"

It was so weird. I mean, she really seemed to care. I decided to spill the story.

"And if we don't catch any fish today, we'll probably get kicked out of the game," Campbell added when I was done.

"Don't worry. You won't get kicked out." Dana smiled. "Hey, I don't have cooking duty for a few more hours. Maybe I can help you catch some fish."

Why is Dana being so nice to us? I wondered. Then I realised that she probably was just doing it because she wanted to win the gift certificate.

In any case, I was glad Dana helped us out. Within a few hours Campbell, Dana and I had caught a ton of fish! We brought them to Seth and Elise so they could start cooking dinner.

"Elise, can I have some water?" Seth asked, holding out his hand.

"Oh, yeah," Elise said, examining her fingernails. "About the water. We don't have any."

"Weren't you supposed to collect it today?" Dana asked.

"Mmm-hmm." Elise shrugged. "But I used it all for something really important."

"What?" Seth asked.

"My hair," Elise replied. She flipped her long brown hair back and forth. "Doesn't it look better now that I washed it?"

I stared openmouthed at Elise. This didn't seem like her at all. She was usually super-responsible.

I'm sure you know what happened next. Elise got kicked out of the game! At least Ashley will have one more person to hang out with.

Everyone was happy with us again at dinner. I expected Dana to stand up and say that she helped us catch the fish, but she didn't say anything. Didn't she want to show off her good teamwork? Why would she help us if she didn't want the credit?

Is it possible that she was just being . . . nice?

Dear Diary,

"Is that the Glittery Grape? Pass it over, will you?"

"Who has Peppermint Pink?"

Summer, Elise and I were giving one another

pedicures in my room to celebrate Elise leaving Wild Hawaii. Our plan totally worked!

Summer and Elise were both in super-good

moods. "This is way better than picking coconuts and berries," Summer said as she carefully painted Elise's toenails.

"Absolutely," Elise agreed. "How did I ever live without a bed?"

"I can't even remember why I was upset for getting kicked out of the game," I added. "I would much rather hang out in the hotel than rough it in a tent on the beach."

"So what should we do tomorrow?" Summer leaned back on a pillow.

Her question gave me an idea. One that I was sure would make my friends even happier!

"Girls, tomorrow is going to be our most fun day yet," I said. "I'm going to have a sleepover in my room to celebrate our freedom."

"Excellent!" Elise gave me a high five. "It's party time!"

Chapter 7

Friday

Dear Diary,

This morning, Campbell and I  offered to collect berries for breakfast. I guess we were hoping to make up for the garbage incident yesterday.

"So what do you want to do on our day off tomorrow?" I asked as we strolled up to the campsite with two full buckets of berries.

"Why don't we go exploring?" Campbell suggested. She plunked down her bucket next to the camp's cooking supplies.

I hesitated. "I'm not sure I want to," I said, placing my bucket next to hers.

"Why not?" Campbell asked.

"Because think of all the bad luck we might have if we did that!" I said. "We could get lost, or get trapped in a cave, or something."

Campbell laughed. "Come on, Mary-Kate," she said. "Nothing else is going to happen to us."

Famous last words, right, Diary? Because when we came back an hour later, the cooking crew was busy making breakfast. And they weren't happy to see us!

"You could have picked more than ten berries,"

Seth pointed out as soon as soon as we walked up.

"What do you mean?" I asked. "We brought you two full buckets."

"The buckets weren't full when we got here," Elise said.

"I don't get it," Campbell said.

"What's going on, gang?" Maleko asked, strolling over to our group.

"Uh, well, we accidentally messed up breakfast," I admitted. I explained the situation.

"Wait a second," Dana said. "Maybe some birds came and ate the berries. That's possible, right?"

"But no birds ever ate any of the food we left out before," Elise said.

"That's because nobody else has our bad luck," I muttered to Campbell. "I told you it wasn't over."

"Bad luck?" Maleko asked. "I warned you, didn't I?" he said, wagging a finger at me.

"Tell me about it," I said as Maleko walked away.

I turned to Campbell. "I think Maleko is right," I said. "Pele is mad because we didn't leave her a gift."

Campbell stared at me in amazement. "Mary-Kate, are you kidding me?"

"I know it sounds weird," I answered, "but how else can you explain all our horrible luck?"

Campbell shrugged. "I don't know. But I'm

pretty sure it has nothing to do with a goddess that lives in a volcano."

"Just to be on the safe side," I said, "how about we hike back to the volcano tomorrow and leave Pele some presents?"

Campbell rolled her eyes. "Oh, all right. If you really want to. Just let me know when we're leaving."

I smiled. I felt better knowing we were going back. I mean, deep down I didn't *really* believe in the curse of Pele. (But just to be on the safe side, I wouldn't mind visiting the volcano again.)

Dear Diary,

Summer, Elise and I had the best time in my room tonight. Summer borrowed a boom box from the front desk so we could play our 4-You CDs. Elise brought all her makeup along so we could give one another makeovers.

Best of all, we knew Jeremy wouldn't crash our party because he was busy watching *Revenge of the Killer Mummies Part Two: Terror in Texas* on cable.

I sat in a chair and studied the room-service menu.

"Check it out, guys," I said, flipping through the

plastic-coated pages. "We can order ten kinds of ice cream in one big bowl!"

Summer turned up the 4-You song that was playing on the radio and bopped over to the chair. "Sounds good to me," she said. "While you're at it, can you order me some cheese fries?"

"And I wouldn't mind some veggies and dip," Elise added.

"Let's rent a movie, too!" Summer suggested. "You can do that just by using the remote control." She pressed some buttons on the TV remote and a really good movie appeared on the screen.

I picked up the phone and gave the man at the front desk our order. I added a few more things from the menu, just in case we were still hungry later on. The man promised to have our food delivered within an hour.

"An hour!" Summer cried. "All this talk about food has made me seriously hungry."

"Me, too," I agreed. My eyes landed on the minifridge underneath the TV. "Hey, what's in there?" I asked.

I peeked inside. "All right!" I cheered. The fridge was stocked with juice, soda and snacks.

Before we knew it, the three of us had eaten it all.

Diary, our party was a blast. We watched the movie, danced, sang and ate until we were stuffed. It was the greatest night ever!

Ring! Ring!

The next morning I woke up to the sound of the phone jangling next to my ear on the bedside table. *Who could be calling me this early?* I wondered. I reached over and picked it up. "Hello?"

"Hello. This is Mr. Kawabata," the voice on the other end of the line said. "I'm the hotel manager."

"Who is it?" Elise called from the next bed. I waved my hand for her to be quiet.

"How can I help you?" I asked in my most polite voice.

"I'm sorry to bother you," Mr. Kawabata said, "but I was going through my computer records and saw that you made a lot of room service charges last night. A few hundred dollars' worth, in fact."

"Um, I guess we were really hungry," I said, not sure what else to say. *Why is he calling to tell me this?* I wondered.

Mr. Kawabata cleared his throat. "I'm not sure your chaperons, Mr. Turnbull and Ms. Clare, made it clear to you. But room service is not part of your vacation package."

"What?" I gulped. Then I had an even worse thought. "How about the minifridge? Is that included?"

"No, I'm afraid it's not," Mr. Kawabata replied. "I'm calling to make sure you will be able to pay the bill."

I almost dropped the phone. There was *no way* we could pay for all the food we ate.

Which meant one thing. We were in big trouble!

Chapter 8

Saturday

Dear Diary,

Elise, Summer and I spent the rest of the morning trying to come up with ways to get the money for our room service bill without Ms. Clare or Mr. Turnbull finding out.

"What are we going to do!" Summer wailed, flopping over on my bed.

Elise hugged a pillow. "If Ms. Clare and Mr. Turnbull find out what we did, we are toast," she added.

"I'm pretty sure our parents won't be too happy with us either," Summer said.

"We have to talk to the manager," I said. "Maybe if we promise we'll never order room service again, he will forget the whole thing."

I didn't believe that one myself, but I was trying to look on the bright side.

I could tell Elise and Summer weren't thrilled with the thought of talking to the manager of the hotel. But what else could we do?

The three of us went downstairs and found Mr. Kawabata's office. I took a deep breath, plastered on my biggest smile, and marched in.

"Good morning, ladies," Mr. Kawabata said, looking up from his desk. "How can I help you?"

"I'm Ashley Burke," I said. "We spoke on the phone this morning."

"Ah, yes, Ms. Burke." Mr. Kawabata shook my hand with an amused smile. "You must be here to discuss your food charges."

"Um, sort of." I looked at Elise and Summer for support, but they seemed ready to run out the door at any second. Then I turned back to Mr. Kawabata. "Um, we don't really have the money to pay our bill," I told him.

"I see," Mr. Kawabata said. "I'm sure your chaperons can settle the bill for now." He picked up the phone.

"Please, Mr. Kawabata. Ms. Clare and Mr. Turnbull can't find out about this," I said. "They'll tell our parents and we'll get in really big trouble!"

"It was a huge mistake," Elise added. "We'll never do it again."

"We promise!" Summer chimed in.

"I'm sorry," Mr. Kawabata said. "But I have no other choice. Your bill has to be settled somehow."

He started to dial the phone.

I glanced around desperately, hoping an answer would fall out of the air. I noticed a cleaning lady pushing her cart past the doorway. That gave me an idea. "Wait!" I cried. "What if we worked at the hotel to pay off our bill?"

Mr. Kawabata hung up the phone. "Hmmm," he said slowly. "I suppose I *could* give you some odd jobs around the hotel. Are you sure you're willing to do that?"

"Definitely," I said. I turned to Elise and Summer. "Right, guys?"

"R-right," Elise and Summer said together. They didn't look as sure as I felt, though.

"Okay then," Mr. Kawabata said.

"Guys, isn't that great?" I asked as we left the manager's office.

"Yeah, terrific," Elise grumbled.

"It's just how I wanted to spend my vacation," Summer added.

"Come on," I said. "So we answer some telephones and make some beds for the next few days. It won't be so bad. Really."

63

Dear Diary,

This morning I woke up bright and  early to hike to the volcano. I headed over to Campbell's tent to wake her up. I met Dana on the way.

"Hi, Mary-Kate," she said. "What are you doing out so early?"

"Campbell and I are going back to the volcano today to leave Pele some gifts," I explained.

"Cool," Dana said. "Do you mind if I come with you?"

I thought about it for a second. Dana wasn't so bad to be around these days. "Why not?" I replied. "We can all go together. I'm just going to wake up Campbell now."

"Oh, I'll get her," Dana said, heading towards Campbell's tent. "That way you can get ready. I'm all set to go."

"Thanks, Dana." I smiled and went back to my tent. Wow. Maybe the Wild Hawaii experience really did bring out the best in people. It sure was working on Dana.

Dana peeked into my tent a few minutes later. She was alone. Her mouth was set in a tight line. "I talked to Campbell about the hike," she said.

"Is she getting ready?" I asked.

"Campbell isn't coming. She said . . ." Dana's voice drifted off.

"What?" I asked. "What did she say?"

"Nothing. Never mind." Dana looked down.

What is it that she doesn't want to tell me? I wondered. "Dana, what did she say?" I repeated.

"Okay, okay." Dana took a deep breath. "Campbell said that you are totally out of control with this whole Pele thing. She's never seen you act so dumb."

I shook my head. "No way," I replied. "Campbell would never say that about me."

"Whatever, Mary-Kate," Dana said. "But that's what she told me."

I was so confused. I know Campbell didn't believe in the legend of Pele. But why would she say such mean things about me? And why would she bail on our plans?

I'll talk to her later, I decided.

"I guess it's just us then," I said, picking up my backpack.

Mr. Turnbull had agreed to come along on our hike to make sure we were okay. Today he was dressed in khaki shorts, orange socks, hiking boots and a T-shirt that said I LOVE HAWAII. He was carrying huge binoculars.

I wanted to get to the volcano as fast as possible. But Mr. Turnbull kept slowing us down. Every few feet he wanted to stop and  study plants and insects. With each stop he would say things like "Excellent specimen of orchid!" or "Superb bromeliad!" Dana and I just rolled our eyes at each other and giggled.

SUPERB BROMELIAD

Along the way Dana and I talked. And talked. And talked. Back at school we never had a real conversation. She definitely seemed different now that we were in Hawaii. And you know what, Diary? I almost like her.

"I can't believe Campbell said you were dumb," Dana commented as we approached the base of the volcano. "Best friends shouldn't talk that way about each other. I know *I* wouldn't talk about my best friend that way."

I shrugged. I didn't want to say anything bad about Campbell. But deep down I felt a pang. Dana was right. Best friends *shouldn't* talk that way about each other.

"I hate to say it, Mary-Kate, but I guess you're just nicer than Campbell is," Dana went on.

I didn't know what to say to that. And I really

didn't want to talk about this any more. "Hey, that's where we found those rocks." I pointed up ahead.

"Let's go," Dana said.

We left Mr. Turnbull behind to inspect some dried lava.

I took off my backpack and opened it. I had no idea what kind of gifts Pele would want so I had brought along a paper clip, a pink hair slide, and a coconut. I figured she would have to like one of them!

I knelt down and laid the gifts on the ground. "There. Do you think my bad luck will go away now?" I asked Dana.

"I'm sure of it!" Dana said, nodding. "Hmm . . . wait a sec, I'll be right back."

She wandered off and returned a few minutes later with a handful of colourful flowers. She put them down on top of my gifts. "There," she said, "now it's perfect. Pele is sure to get over her grumpy mood when she sees these!"

I laughed. "Come on, we'd better get back," I said. "It's almost time to start our chores."

We headed down the trail, picking up Mr. Turnbull along the way. It was a breezy day. Big colourful birds swooped down over us as we hiked. I felt as if a huge weight had lifted off my shoulders.

 I could tell – my luck was beginning to change already!

"I'm so glad we went to the volcano," I told Dana as we neared the camp. "Thanks for coming with me."

"No problem," Dana said, grinning. "After all, what are friends for?"

Friends? Me and Dana Woletsky? A week ago I wouldn't have thought that was possible.

But maybe I just didn't know the real Dana, Diary.

Chapter 9

Sunday

Dear Diary,

How bad could working in the hotel be? I'll tell you how bad it could be! Worse than I ever thought!

"Where are the Band-Aids?" Summer asked as she ran past me at the pool.

I peeked out from behind the enormous tray of food I was carrying. "In the white cabinet. Do you remember if we have guava smoothies on the menu?" I asked. "The lady at table five wants one."

"I'm not sure," Summer replied. "We have ten kinds. Mango . . . and, uh, nine other ones."

"Oh, well. I'll figure it out." I turned around and knocked right into Elise, who was speeding the other way.

Crash! My tray fell to the floor.

"Oh, no!" I cried.

"If people need crisps and salsa so badly, why can't they get up and get it themselves?" Elise cried. "I'm busy!"

Uh-oh, I thought. *She has totally lost it.*

"Is there a problem?" Mr. Kawabata asked, walking over to us.

"No problem at all," I said, quickly piling the dishes back onto the tray.

"Good," he replied. "Because those people on the lounge chairs would like a pineapple smoothie, table three needs their lunch order, and the lifeguards are asking for more sunscreen."

Elise, Summer, and I all sighed at the same time. Then we took off again.

By the middle of the afternoon, the three of us had had it. We plopped down on some lounge chairs by the pool to take a break.

"This is torture," Summer complained.

"Did we have to eat *everything* in the minifridge?" Elise groaned.

"Look at it this way," I said. "At least we didn't get in trouble for anything. And our bill is already half paid."

Summer and Elise scowled at me.

I sat forward in my chair. "Okay, you're right. This is the pits. Even Wild Hawaii is better than this!"

"Do you really think so?" a voice behind me said.

I whipped around. It was Ms. Clare! She was dressed in a flowered muumuu and sandals.

"Uh-oh," I muttered. How much of our conversation had she heard?

Apparently not that much, since Ms. Clare sat down on my lounge chair and smiled at the three of us.

"I feel terrible that you girls aren't participating in Wild Hawaii anymore," she said. "And I'm sorry you don't like hanging out at the hotel."

"That's okay," I said slowly. Ms. Clare had obviously misunderstood our conversation. She thought we were saying that lounging at the hotel wasn't as fun as being in Wild Hawaii!

"No, it's not okay," Ms. Clare went on. "I'm going to make sure you girls get involved again."

"You are?" Summer asked warily.

Ms. Clare nodded. "Maleko was just saying this morning that he needed some extra help around the camp. I'll bet you three would be perfect for the job!"

A bad feeling swirled in the pit of my stomach. "Help?" I echoed. "What kind of help?"

"I'm not sure," Ms. Clare said. "But just think – you'll get to go back to camp and see all your friends again!"

"What about Jeremy?" I asked. "Is he going, too?"

Ms. Clare shook her head. "No. Jeremy seems very happy at the hotel."

"Oh," I said.

"So it's settled then," Ms. Clare said. "Starting today, you're back on part-time duty for Wild Hawaii. Come on, let's go over to the camp right now."

The three of us dragged ourselves off the lounge chairs and followed Ms. Clare to the Wild Hawaii camp.

"Nice to see you," Maleko said when we arrived at camp.

"The girls really missed Wild Hawaii," Ms. Clare explained, "so they came back to help out."

"That's the team spirit I'm looking for!" Maleko said. "Why don't you start by picking some berries? And when you're finished with that, you can refill the water bottles."

"Great," I said, smiling tightly. All I could think about was that we still had to go back to the hotel and finish our work there!

So now we have two jobs instead of one, Diary. And it's all because of me and my big mouth.

72

Island Girls

Dear Diary,

I don't know if it has anything to do with my visit to the volcano, but nothing has gone wrong all morning. I hope this is a sign for what the rest of the day is going to be like!

Today we're going to another exciting place – a three-hundred-foot waterfall! The name of the waterfall is Umauma.

As we began our hike to the beach, I started to make my way over to Campbell. I wanted to ask her why she didn't come to the volcano. But Dana grabbed my arm and asked if we could walk together.

"Um, sure," I replied. She was so nice yesterday. How could I say no?

We started gabbing about our trip to the volcano. Just as we were cracking up about Mr. Turnbull, Campbell brushed past me on the trail.

"Oh, hey, Campbell." I smiled at her. "I was looking for you before. Do you want to hang out with us?"

Campbell glanced at Dana, then at me. "No. I told Julia I'd hang with her." She walked ahead.

Was it me, Diary, or did Campbell seem really mad at me? What did I do?

"Nice talking to you, Campbell," Dana said

sarcastically. "Hey, Mary-Kate, check out that lizard over there!"

As we hiked, I kept wondering why Campbell was acting so strangly. *Maybe she is just in a bad mood or something*, I thought.

Pretty soon we reached the waterfall. Exotic birds swooped through the air.

"Those are *anianiau* and white-footed boobies," Maleko pointed out. The water tumbled over rock formations and landed in a big emerald-coloured pool. There were tiny rainbows in the air from where the sunlight hit the drops of water as they fell.

I saw Campbell standing alone by the waterfall. I decided to go over and talk to her.

"Pretty cool beach, huh?" I asked.

"Whatever," Campbell said, not looking at me.

What is wrong with her? I wondered. "Soooo, when do you want to go fishing today?" I tried again.

Campbell turned her back on me completely. "Maybe you should go fishing with Dana instead," she suggested. "I don't feel like going." She walked away.

I was speechless. *What just happened here?* I

thought. *First Campbell is acting all mean to me and now she doesn't want to talk to me at all?*

I guess my bad luck hasn't gone away, Diary. Because what could be worse luck than not getting along with your best friend – and not knowing why?

Chapter 10

Monday

Dear Diary,

What was Campbell's problem? I tossed and turned last night in my tent, trying to figure out why she was acting so strangely.

Well, whatever it was, I wanted to fix it as soon as possible. I wasn't sure if she would talk to me, so I decided to write her a note.

Dear Campbell,

I'm not sure why you don't want to hang out with me any more. But if I did something to make you angry, I'm sorry! Can we talk about it and figure things out? You're my best friend.

Love,
Mary-Kate

I read it and reread it. Then I decided to leave some pretty flowers with the note.

I hiked to a spot near the

beach where lots of different-coloured flowers grew. I started picking a few of them when I heard a familiar voice behind me.

"Hey, Mary-Kate!"

I turned around. It was Dana.

"Hey," I said. "What's going on?"

"Not much," she replied. "What are you doing?"

I told her about what had happened with Campbell. Then I mentioned how I wanted to leave the flowers for her, along with an apology note.

"That is so sweet," Dana said enthusiastically. "Where are you going to leave it?"

"In her tent," I said. "That way she won't miss it."

Dana nodded. "Campbell *has* to talk to you after that," she said. "Want me to help you pick some flowers?"

I never thought I'd say this, but I'm kind of glad I had Dana around. She really made me feel better. A few minutes later, I left a huge bunch of flowers on top of Campbell's sleeping bag, along with the note.

I was sure that once Campbell saw them she would forgive me.

Two of a Kind Diaries

Dear Diary,

The nightmare continues.

This morning, Summer, Elise and I were back at the hotel, waiting on the guests at the pool. Then this afternoon we were back at camp, doing more chores. And to make things worse, Phoebe was videotaping us for her documentary the entire time we were at camp. Now everyone back at school would see us all gross and covered with dirt!

One bright spot about being at camp is that I get to see Mary-Kate. She was totally psyched when we ran into each other after lunch.

"What are you *doing* here?" she shrieked, hugging me.

I explained the whole horrible story.

"That's awful," Mary-Kate said. "But I have to tell you something even worse! Campbell doesn't want to be my friend anymore."

"What?" I exclaimed. "Did you have a huge fight with her or something?"

"Not really." Mary-Kate sighed. "She just won't talk to me. I left her a note and some flowers today, but she hasn't said anything about it."

"Maybe she just didn't see them yet," I said.

"Mary-Kate! Time to get going!" Maleko called.

"Give me an update later," I said.

Mary-Kate nodded and ran off to join the rest of the group.

I sighed and trudged down to the spring with a bucket. I felt really bad for Mary-Kate. Why would Campbell act so weird?

As I dipped the bucket into the water, I overheard a conversation coming from a nearby patch of trees. *Ooh, maybe it's some good gossip to share with Elise and Summer*, I thought. The sound of a small waterfall nearby was making it hard to hear who was talking so I leaned in to listen.

"I *thought* she was my friend, but I'm not so sure anymore," a girl's voice said.

"How come?" a second girl asked.

"You think she's loyal, but she's not what she seems."

Wow, I thought. *Whoever they're talking about sounds like bad news.*

"I never would have thought that about her," the second girl replied.

"Well, believe it," the first girl said. "Mary-Kate is not the person people think she is."

They were talking about my sister! I had to find out who it was.

I walked closer to the voices and peeked around a tree.

I blinked and blinked. I couldn't believe it. It was Julia and Campbell, sitting on a rock by the waterfall.

"I don't think I want to be her friend anymore," Campbell said.

I gasped. *Campbell* was the one talking about Mary-Kate!

Chapter 11

Tuesday

Dear Diary,

I was so upset when Ashley told me  the horrible things that Campbell said about me. When I was finished being upset I started getting angry. So much that I refused to be in the same place as Campbell the entire day.

But once the afternoon rolled around, there was no getting past it – we were teammates. I had to go fishing with her.

I strolled up to the boat. Campbell was already there, putting some minnows into a bucket. My chest felt really tight. How was I going to get through this?

"I thought you didn't want to go fishing with me," I said, crossing my arms.

 "I'm just trying to be a team player," Campbell said.

Then I noticed that my fishing pole wasn't where I had left it. Campbell's was right there in the boat.

"Campbell," I said. "Have you seen my fishing pole?"

"No," she replied. "Is it missing?"

"Yeah." I shrugged. *Maybe I took it back to my tent*

or something, I thought. "I'm going to find it," I said. "I'll be right back."

I trudged back to the campsite and searched my tent. Nope. No fishing pole. *Where could it be?* I wondered.

I hunted around camp a bit and then gave up. I was going to have to tell Campbell we were fishing with one pole today.

I headed back to the rowing boat. On the way, I noticed something pointy sticking out of Campbell's tent.

That's weird, I thought. *It's shaped just like . . .*

I glanced around to make sure no one was watching me. Then I knelt down and unzipped the flap.

I gasped. My fishing pole was lying across Campbell's sleeping bag!

Now I was really angry. Campbell had hidden my fishing pole on purpose. Why? Because she didn't want me to go fishing with her?

"What are you doing in my tent?"

I whipped around. Campbell was standing behind me with her arms folded across her chest.

I held up my fishing pole. "Why is my fishing

pole in your tent?" I asked. "You said you didn't know where it was."

Campbell's jaw dropped. "I didn't! I have no idea how it got there."

"Yeah, right," I shot back. "Then why did you come back to the campsite just now? I'll bet it was to make sure I didn't find it!"

"That's not true!" Campbell shook her head. "I was coming to help you."

I turned away from Campbell. "You're lying," I said.

"H-how can you say that?" Campbell sputtered.

I faced her again. "I can't trust anything you say these days."

Campbell's lower lip trembled. "Fine!" she shouted. "If that's what you think, then I don't want to be friends any more!" Campbell took off running.

"*Fine!*" I shouted back.

But it wasn't fine. I was angry with Campbell, but the last thing I wanted was to lose my best friend.

Dear Diary,

Tomorrow is the last day of Wild Hawaii. If you ask me, the whole trip has been a major disaster in the friendship department. Summer, Elise and I are not having any fun together at all. And at camp this morning Mary-Kate told me about her blow-out fight with Campbell.

Mary-Kate was really upset. "I just don't know how this happened," she said in a shaky voice as we sat together on the beach. "Campbell said she hadn't seen my fishing pole, but there it was – sticking out of her tent!"

"That doesn't sound like Campbell at all," I said. Then I thought back to the nasty things I had heard Campbell say about Mary-Kate.

"You wouldn't believe it, Ashley," Mary-Kate said, "but the person who has been helping me through this, besides you, is Dana!"

"Dana who?" I asked. There was no way my sister was talking about Dana Woletsky!

"I know it sounds crazy," Mary-Kate said, "but Dana and I are kind of friends now."

"How did that happen?" I asked.

Mary-Kate shrugged. "I'm not really sure. All I know is that she's not the person we thought she was. I bet you would like her, too, if you got to know her."

"I'm not so sure about that one," I pointed out. "What about the time she tried to steal my boyfriend, Ross? Or when she tried to lose that

sports tournament in Florida just because I was
team captain? She's really mean, Mary-Kate."

"I know, but she's different now," Mary-Kate
explained. "I think Wild Hawaii really changed her."

"Ummmm, if you say so," I said. But secretly there
was no way I believed Dana could be that different.

Mary-Kate sighed. "But I don't want to talk
about Dana. I want to talk about Campbell. Do you
think she is telling the truth?" Mary-Kate asked.

"I don't know," I said. "We need to find out
what's really going on around here."

"How?" Mary-Kate asked, sniffling.

I stood up and brushed some sand off my shorts.
"When I'm done working here, I'll do a little
snooping around and see what I can
find out."

"Thanks, Ashley," Mary-Kate replied.
"You are the greatest sister in the
world!"

I grinned. "I know, I know." I was
happy to help out Mary-Kate. That's
what sisters are for!

I stifled a yawn as I helped Mary-Kate to her feet.
Diary, I'm probably the only person ever to come to
Hawaii on vacation – and end up working as a
waitress, dishwasher, towel girl and spy!

Chapter 12

Thursday

Dear Diary,

This is the last day of our Wild Hawaii adventure. I'm not exactly sure when it got this bad – but teamwork has reached an all-time low.

Campbell and I decided to fish at different times during the day, so we wouldn't have to see each other. Once everyone else noticed we weren't getting along, their teamwork kind of slacked off, too.

Seth complained that he had to cook and collect food now that Summer and Jeremy were gone. Grant and Julia fought over who should carry more firewood. And Maleko was not happy about any of it.

The only person who has stayed neutral through all of this . . . is Dana!

"All right, people!" she said this morning after breakfast. "Just because this is the last day of Wild Hawaii doesn't mean we can all stop working. We still have to collect food for lunch, get more fresh water, and start packing up our stuff. Come on, team, move!"

Everyone grumbled and slowly got to their

feet. Then we all started our chores.

"Thank you, Dana," Maleko said, smiling. "It's nice to see someone still remembers what teamwork is."

Who would have thought that Dana would be the one trying to pull the group together? I guess you just never know about people.

Dear Diary,

We're almost done! Even though we finished our work at the hotel a few days ago, Maleko put Elise, Summer and me in charge of combing the campsite to make sure we didn't leave anything behind. So we're still hard at work.

"Hey, guys!" I told my friends as I pulled a stake out of the ground. "Think of it this way. If we hadn't done all this work outside we wouldn't be as totally buff and tan as we are right now. We look just like personal trainers."

Summer glanced at her tanned arms. A smile spread across her face. "I like the sound of that!" she said.

I had a special surprise for Elise. "Hey, Elise, you'll never believe what I learned," I said, picking a flower and holding it out to her. "If you rub this on your skin, your skin will automatically sparkle!"

"Really?" Elise said, taking the flower. She loves *anything* with glitter and sparkles.

Yay! I had managed to make both my friends happy!

That is, until Phoebe came over with her video camera. "I'm interviewing everyone for last-day thoughts," she explained, zooming in on us. "Elise, what do you have to say about Wild Hawaii?"

Elise's smile vanished. "I want to go home," she grumbled, dropping some tools into a box.

"I don't need to go home," Summer said into the camera. "I just really need a manicure!" She held out a hand with five broken fingernails.

"Maybe we need a break," I suggested. Then I eyed Phoebe's video camera. "Hey, Phoebe, did you interview Campbell yet?"

"No, why?" Phoebe asked.

"Can I do it for you?" I asked. "I'm a whiz with a video camera. And you can take a break, too."

Phoebe shrugged. "Okay." She handed me the camera.

Perfect, I thought. *Now I'll have an excuse to talk to*

Campbell about Mary-Kate. I said good-bye to my friends and walked off in search of Campbell.

As I got closer to the trees, I heard a girl talking. "Maleko is sure to give me that hundred-dollar gift certificate for best teamwork now," she said. It was Dana!

I peeked from behind a tree. Dana was leaning against a palm branch talking on a mobile phone.

"I can't believe I pulled it off, Kristen!" she said. "First I got Mary-Kate and Campbell to argue. Then I got everyone else fighting, too!"

I bet she's talking to Kristen Lindquist, I thought. Kristen was her best friend at White Oak.

I slinked around a few trees and rocks until I could see Dana, but I made sure she couldn't see me. I held up the video camera and pressed the Record button.

"I knew they were my worst competition for the gift certificate," Dana went on. "So I made them think that they were cursed by dumping their bait and oars into the lagoon. Then when Mary-Kate 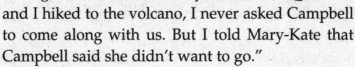 and I hiked to the volcano, I never asked Campbell to come along with us. But I told Mary-Kate that Campbell said she didn't want to go."

I was burning with anger. Mary-Kate was so wrong about Dana. Wild Hawaii hadn't changed her at all.

Dana giggled. "But the best was when I made sure Campbell never got this apology note Mary-Kate wrote her – and then I made it seem like Campbell stole Mary-Kate's fishing pole!"

Keep talking, I thought, as I zoomed the camera in on her. *Keep talking!*

Dana rocked back and forth with laughter. "I know. I was sure that if I acted really friendly with Mary-Kate, Campbell would get jealous. Am I good, or what?"

I'd heard enough. I clicked off the video camera and tiptoed away.

Chapter 13

Thursday

Dear Diary,

Around four o'clock, Maleko gathered the group one last time. He wanted to make his announcement about the winner for best teamwork. We all sat in a circle at the centre of camp, waiting for him to speak.

"Okay," he said. "First of all, I hope you had fun at Wild Hawaii. You challenged yourselves every day and you should be proud of what you've accomplished here."

Everyone clapped.

Phoebe leaned over to me. "Ashley, can I have my video camera back?" she asked. "I should probably get this on tape."

"Just a sec," I whispered. "I need it for something really important."

"I'm sure you're dying to know," Maleko went on, "so let me cut to the chase and announce the winner of the Best Teamwork prize."

Everyone seemed pretty down in the dumps when Maleko said that. I could tell most of the group thought they hadn't been very good team players towards the end. But Dana was sitting up straight and smiling.

Maleko held up the gift certificate. "The winner for best teamwork is – Dana Woletsky!"

Dana stood up and flipped her dark brown hair over her shoulders. "Thank you so much!" she said, waving at everyone as if she were on a parade float or something. "I had such a great time with you all."

Oh, give me a break, I thought, and jumped to my feet.

"Wait a second," I said, holding out the video camera. "Can we watch this tape first?"

Dana stopped waving and glared at me. "Give it up, Ashley," she said. "You don't have to act jealous just because you got kicked out on the first day."

"What do you want to show us?" Maleko asked. He didn't seem to have much patience, so I rewound the tape and pressed Play.

Maleko and the other kids gathered around to watch the little screen on the video camera. The image of Dana talking on her cell phone appeared.

Dana gasped. "When did you tape that?"

I smiled at her and turned up the volume. Dana's recorded voice rang out. "Maleko is sure to give me that hundred-dollar gift certificate for best teamwork now . . . But the best was when I made sure Campbell never got this apology note that Mary-Kate wrote her – and then I made it seem like Campbell stole Mary-Kate's fishing pole!"

"Stop!" Dana cried out. She turned to Maleko. "Ashley made that up! She faked it somehow. It's all because she hates me!"

Mary-Kate broke through the crowd and marched right up to Dana. "How *could* you!" she cried. "You pretended to be my friend, but you really just wanted to win the prize."

Campbell walked up behind Mary-Kate. Her cheeks were all red. "You're not going to get away with this," she said, pointing a finger in Dana's face. I pressed the Off button and handed the video camera to Maleko. It was game over for Dana Woletsky!

Dear Diary,

How could I have fallen for it? How could I not have  realised that Dana is a big fat liar? She actually made me believe that she was a better friend than Campbell was! And remember the garbage incident and the missing berries? Those were all thanks to Dana, too!

But on a happier note, now that the truth is out, I'm sure everything will be fine between Campbell and me again. As soon as I finish writing in you, Diary, I'm going to find her. I can't wait to make up!

Chapter 14

Friday

Dear Diary,

You will never guess what happened next. After all the excitement died down, a bunch of us decided to hang out by the pool at the hotel. Maleko came strolling over, holding the gift certificate in his hand.

"I've made my decision about the new winner for best teamwork," he announced.

Everyone stopped talking. Mary-Kate leaned over from the chair next to me. "I wonder who it's going to be," she whispered.

"Me, too," I whispered back. "Hey, maybe it's you!"

Mary-Kate shrugged. "I doubt it."

Maleko held up the gift certificate. "The winner is . . . Ashley Burke!" He looked straight at me.

I turned around. I figured there must have been another Ashley Burke sitting behind me, because there was no way Maleko was talking about me. I got kicked out of the game on day one!

"Yes, I mean you, Ashley," Maleko said, laughing at my reaction. "You deserve the prize."

"Why?" I asked, still confused.

Maleko handed the certificate to me. "Even though you made a mistake early on and had to leave the game, you more than made up for it by coming back to pitch in and bringing Summer and Elise with you."

"Wow, thanks!" I cried. Can you believe it, Diary?

Everyone came up to me and gave me high fives and big hugs. I went straight over to Summer and Elise.

"What do you say we all go on a Hawaiian shopping spree together?" I suggested. "We can split the prize three ways."

Elise's eyes lit up. "Thanks, Ashley."

Summer grinned. "Awesome!"

Isn't that excellent? Right after we left the pool, we went to the hotel boutiques. Summer chose a jar of pineapple facial cream, Elise bought a sparkly Hawaiian baby tee, and I got a new pair of cool-looking sunglasses. We all picked out a bunch of other souvenirs, too.

"I'm going to wear these for the next part of our Hawaiian vacation," I told Summer and Elise, slipping on my shades.

"We're going to a resort on another island. Kauai, right?" Summer said.

I nodded. "Right. And do you know what that means?"

Elise frowned. "What?"

I threw my arms into the air. "No more work!"

We all giggled like crazy as we left the store with a bunch of shopping bags.

My vacation in Hilo is going to have a happy ending after all! I thought.

Or maybe not. Leave it to Dana to burst my bubble. She approached me in the lobby right after Summer and Elise headed back to their room. "I need to talk to you," she said in a low voice.

"What do you want?" I asked. I was still angry at Dana for what she did to Mary-Kate.

Dana gave me a mean smile. "You ruined my trip. So now I'm going to ruin yours."

"What are you talking about?" I narrowed my eyes.

"I know a big secret about you," Dana said, smoothing down her pink skirt. "And when I tell everyone what it is, your vacation will be over."

I froze. "What secret?" I asked her, glancing around.

"You'll find out soon enough," Dana said. With that, she laughed and sauntered away.

What was she talking about? Did she really know something, or was she just lying again?

Dear Diary,

Diary, I have a HUGE problem!

Actually, *two* huge problems!

Now that Wild Hawaii is over and Ashley uncovered Dana's big plan, I thought that everything would be fine between Campbell and me.

But it's not.

Campbell didn't talk to me at all last night. She didn't talk to me this morning either. Every time I tried to speak to her, she made herself busy doing something else.

I didn't get it. "Campbell," I said as I watched her pack her suitcase. "I'm really really sorry about what happened. I should have never listened to Dana. Can't you accept my apology so we can be best friends again?"

Campbell slammed her suitcase shut and glared at me. "No, I can't," she said coldly. "You accused me of stealing, and there's no excuse for that! There's also no excuse for believing all those awful things Dana said about me. Friends would never do that to each other – and *definitely* not best friends!"

She picked up her suitcase and headed for the door. "Sit with someone else on the boat, okay? And find someone else to share a room with in Kauai. Our friendship is history."

Diary, what am I going to do? I have to make Campbell forgive me!

Oh, and then there's my other problem.

Dana told Ashley that she knows a secret about her – one that's going to ruin her trip. Ashley doesn't know whether to believe her or not.

But I do. Dana is telling the truth. And the reason I know that is because . . . I'm the one who told her the secret!

What am I going to do?

mary-kateandashley

Surf, Sand,
and Secrets

by Nancy Butcher

from the series created by Robert Griffard
& Howard Adler

HarperCollins*Entertainment*
An Imprint of HarperCollins*Publishers*

A PARACHUTE PRESS BOOK

Chapter 1

Friday

Dear Diary,

Oops! Sorry about that. I didn't mean for you to get splashed. I've never written in you while I was on a yacht before. Actually, I've never even *been* on a yacht before! It's so cool!

A group of us from the White Oak Academy for Girls are here on a special school trip. That includes my sister, Mary-Kate, and a bunch of our friends from our class from the First Form. Diary, I'll never understand why they don't just call it the seventh grade. Oh, well . . .

A few of the boys from our brother school, Harrington, are here with us, including my weird and annoying cousin Jeremy Burke. Right now he's trying to catch fish off the back of the yacht. He said he couldn't wait for lunch.

I'm sitting at a table on the top deck, so I have a perfect view of everything. We're cruising through Hanalei Bay near the island of Kauai. That's one of the islands of Hawaii. We're on our way to Part Two of our summer vacation at the Hanalei Beach Resort!

Part One was spent in Hilo, which is on a different Hawaiian island. We played a survival game called Wild Hawaii, in which we had to live on the beach for twelve whole days.

Well, maybe not twelve days for me. I kind of got booted from Wild Hawaii on the very first day for not following the rules. Luckily my friends Elise Van Hook and Summer Sorenson got kicked out (accidentally on purpose) right after I did.

"I love this yacht!" my roommate, Phoebe Cahill, cried. She was sitting next to me and filming Elise and Summer, who were leaning against the ship's rail and waving.

Phoebe's been recording our whole trip. She says it's good experience since her dream is to be a journalist.

"Pssst. Ashley."

I glanced up. Dana Woletsky was leaning toward me from the next table. *This can't be good*, I thought. Dana isn't what I would call "a nice person."

"I was just thinking about the juicy secret I know about you," Dana said with a smirk.

I had no idea what Dana was talking about, but I could feel my cheeks turning red anyway. "What secret?" I asked.

"Don't worry," Dana said. "You'll find out soon enough." Her smirk turned into a big smile. "And you're going to get in so much trouble. I can't wait!" She tossed her shiny dark hair and turned back around to her own table.

I wasn't sure if Dana *really* knew a secret about me. You can never tell with her. Maybe she was just saying that so I'd be worried for the rest of the trip.

I think she's still angry that I won a hundred-dollar shopping spree in Hilo. You see, Diary, I volunteered at Wild Hawaii to help with chores even after I got kicked out. Our guide was so impressed he gave me a prize for teamwork!

Well, I'm not going to have time to worry about Dana. There's too much fun planned!

"Ashley, want to check out the resort's brochure?" Mary-Kate pulled a chair up to our table. She gave me a little smile, but I could tell that she wasn't exactly happy. She's bummed because she and her best friend, Campbell Smith, had a fight in Hilo. I hope they make up soon.

"Sure," I said, taking the booklet.

Phoebe leaned over my shoulder. "Look!" she said. "They have hula dancing! Hey, maybe I'll get to wear a grass skirt – just like Elvis Presley in my favorite movie, *Blue Hawaii*."

I giggled. Phoebe loved old movies. In fact, she loved anything vintage. At the moment she was wearing an orange 1950s bathing suit with a big yellow flower on one shoulder.

Elise brushed back her long brown hair. "Well, I can't wait to go surfing," she piped up.

"I'm already an expert surfer," Hans Jensen called over from the next table.

Hans is good at almost every sport. He lets everyone know it, too.

"I can't wait to try wave running," Mary-Kate said.

I smiled. "I'm going to try *all* those things," I said. "This is going to be an awesome week."

I looked at Summer, who was now sitting next to Hans. "Summer, what are you going to do first?"

But Summer didn't seem to hear me. She had her head buried in a magazine.

"Earth to Summer. Come in, Summer," I joked.

"Huh?" Summer's blonde head snapped up.

"What are you reading?" I asked.

Summer held up the latest issue of *The National Inquisitor*. "I am so freaked out. There's the creepiest article in here."

"What's it about?" Mary-Kate asked.

"Aliens," Summer said. She leaned forward. "It says that just last week aliens were spotted hovering over Kauai. That's the island our resort is on!"

She pointed to a fuzzy picture of something that looked like a lit-up spaceship. It was hovering over a few palm trees. The headline read ALOHA, ALIENS!

A bunch of kids gathered around to look at the picture.

"Whoa," Julia Langstrom said.

"Cool!" Grant Marino added.

I rolled my eyes. They didn't really believe in this stuff, did they? I mean, the picture was a total fake.

"It says here that the aliens left a trail of purple shells along the beach," Summer added in a hushed voice. "And the trail pointed straight towards"– she gulped – "the Hanalei Beach Resort!"

I almost burst out laughing. What a joke!

"Hey, my cousin saw a spaceship when he was on vacation in Nevada," Seth Samuels said.

"Really? What did it look like?" Phoebe asked, putting down her video camera. She actually looked interested.

I frowned at my roommate. Why was she even asking something like that? Maybe she was just playing along. Or maybe it was because she was a journalist – always asking questions.

"It was spinning around and had lots of blinking lights," Seth replied. "You know. The usual."

Summer nodded seriously. "We see aliens back home in California all the time." She shuddered. "My friend's brother's surfing buddy almost got abducted once. They tried to take him right out of the water."

Everyone gasped.

"How can you guys believe in UFOs?" I asked.

Summer stared at me. "Ashley, the proof is right in front of your eyes!" She tapped a hot-pink fingernail at the article.

"Whatever you say, Summer." I sat back and folded my arms. "But I'm telling you. There's no such thing as aliens."

Dear Diary,

Here's the deal. I *want* to be happy at this resort. It's totally amazing. But how can I be happy when Campbell isn't speaking to me? She's not only been my roommate since the very first day Ashley and I arrived at White Oak, she's been my best friend!

We'd stay up for hours laughing and talking

about every subject on the face of the earth. She's actually the first girl I've met who knows more about baseball than I do.

And now she hates me because I made a stupid mistake.

"Is this place awesome or what?" Ashley asked as we walked into the huge lobby of the Hanalei Beach Resort.

I sighed. I knew Ashley was trying really hard to cheer me up, but it wasn't working.

"Did you catch the gigantic swimming pool and that amazing beach with the killer waves?" Ashley went on. "And that garden we just passed is incredible. It must have a million different kinds of tropical flowers in it!"

"Mmm-hmm," I said, staring at the floor.

Ashley looked at me sympathetically. "Hey, Mary-Kate, I know you're upset about Campbell. Do you want to talk about it?"

"I just don't know what to do," I said. "She ignored me the entire boat ride. She was too busy hanging out with her new best friend, Julia."

"Well, didn't you guys get to talk before we left Hilo?" Ashley asked.

"Barely," I said. "Just enough for her to tell me she doesn't want to speak to me . . . ever again."

"No way!" Ashley replied. "You guys are best buds. I can't believe she won't forgive you."

"I just wish I could take it all back," I said miserably. After all, I *did* do something really horrible to Campbell.

Back at Wild Hawaii, Dana Woletsky pretended to be my friend and told me a whole bunch of lies about Campbell. She even made it look as if Campbell had stolen something from me.

Dana was so convincing that I believed everything she said. And then I accused Campbell of being a thief and a liar.

"I apologised to Campbell a million times," I told my sister. "But I guess I can't blame her for being so angry."

"What are you going to do?" Ashley asked.

"I haven't figured that out yet," I answered, plopping into a chair near the front desk.

"Well, I'm going to check out the magazines in the gift shop," Ashley said. "Maybe we'll find the answer in an advice column or something." She walked over and pulled a magazine off the rack.

I glanced around the lobby, looking for Campbell. I didn't see her. A tall, good-looking man with short black hair passed by me. He had a fluffy white cat in his arms.

Hey, wait a minute! He looked just like . . .

"Oh, wow!" I cried. I jumped up and ran to my sister. "Ashley, do you see who that is?" I asked, tugging on her arm.

She glanced up from the magazine and wrinkled her nose. "Nope. I give up. Who is it?"

"It's Jake Nakamoto," I said. "One of the coolest, most amazing baseball players in the world!"

"Oh," Ashley replied. She went back to reading the magazine.

Okay, so maybe Ashley wasn't impressed by famous sports stars. But I was. And I knew someone else who would be, too. Campbell!

I scanned the lobby until I found her. She was jumping up and down, trying to see Jake over the huge crowd that was suddenly forming around him. Julia was with her.

Three beefy bodyguards waved the fans away from Jake. "Sorry, folks. Mr. Nakamoto is not signing autographs while he's at the resort," one of the guards said firmly. "No exceptions!"

Gee, that's harsh, I thought, frowning. I hurried over to Campbell.

"Jake Nakamoto is my number one favourite baseball player," she was telling Julia.

"Mine, too," I put in. "Can you believe he's staying here?"

Campbell glanced at me, then turned back to Julia. "Jake's batting average was .350 last year. Impressive, huh? And he hit thirty home runs!"

Okay, okay. I got the message. Campbell was ignoring me. But I wasn't going to give up.

"Hey, Campbell, remember when Jake hit that game-winning home run against Atlanta last season?" I asked.

This time she didn't even look at me.

"See that cat he's carrying? Her name is Snowball," Campbell explained to Julia. "Jake never goes anywhere without her. She's like his good-luck charm."

"Wow, you know a lot about Jake," Julia said.

"Yeah. I sure wish I could have his autograph for my collections," Campbell sighed. "It's such a bummer that he's not signing any."

A lightbulb went off in my head. *That's it!* I thought excitedly. *I'll get Jake Nakamoto's autograph for Campbell. She'll have to forgive me after that. We'll be best friends again for sure!*

There was only one problem. . .

I glanced back at the tough-looking bodyguards surrounding Jake. How would I get past *them*?

Chapter 2

Saturday

Dear Diary,

This morning us grommets were  stoked to tackle those gnarly swells! (That's surfing lingo for we had our first lesson today!)

"Remember to lie flat on the board while you paddle in the water," our instructor, Lani, told us. "Ashley, you're up next."

No problem, I thought. I strapped on my life jacket. Then I lay on my board and paddled away from the beach. A few minutes later a humongous wave rushed toward me. I gulped.

"What do I do now?" I yelled to Lani.

"Try to float over the wave," Lani called.

"Okay!" I moved my arms as quickly as I could and tilted up the nose of the board.

"Uh-oh," I said. The board kept rising up, and up, and up until . . .

 *Crash!* It flipped over and I went under the water. I popped up a second later.

Jeremy pointed at me from the shore. "Hey, Ashley! You got thrashed!" He laughed.

So what if I wiped out? I thought I did pretty well for my first time out.

"Good try!" Lani called. "Come on back now, Ashley."

I climbed onto the board again and paddled to the beach. I headed over to Mary-Kate and Phoebe, who were on the sand, catching rays.

"You okay, Ashley?" Mary-Kate asked.

I dropped my board on the sand and peeled a piece of seaweed off my leg. "Yeah. It was fun up until the wiping-out part."

"I wish we could stay in Hawaii forever." Phoebe sighed. Today she was wearing a bathing suit from the 1940s. It was really cute – navy blue with big white polka dots and a little pleated skirt.

"Me, too," I agreed, staring out at the clear blue ocean.

"I guess it's too bad you'll have to go home early, Ashley," Dana said behind me.

I turned around. Dana was in an expensive black tankini and designer shades.

"Sorry to disappoint you, Dana, but I'm not going anywhere," I replied.

Dana smiled. "If you say so." She wiggled her fingers at me and walked away.

"What was *that* about?" Phoebe asked.

"Dana thinks she knows some deep, dark secret about me." I shook my head. "She's really starting to get on my nerves. I mean, so what if I won the shopping spree. Get over it already."

"Don't worry, Ashley," Phoebe said. "I bet Dana's just messing with you."

Mary-Kate cleared her throat. "Actually, I'm not so sure about that."

I raised my eyebrows. "You're not?"

Mary-Kate bit her lip. She always does that when she doesn't want to tell me something. "See, uh, well . . . Dana *does* know a little something about you."

"Like *what*?" I asked. Then I narrowed my eyes. "And how do you know that?"

Mary-Kate turned bright red. "Because, um, I might be the one who told it to her."

Dear Diary,

I didn't think even Dana would stoop this low, but obviously I was wrong. Well, now it was totally time for me to come clean. I had kept the truth from Ashley for way too long.

I took a deep breath. "Remember how I thought Dana was my friend during Wild Hawaii?" I began.

"Yeeees," Ashley said slowly.

I sighed. "Well, we hung out a lot and told each other all kinds of stuff."

"Stuff like what?" Ashley asked, tapping her foot in the sand.

I hesitated. "Well . . ."

"Come on, Mary-Kate. Spill it now," Ashley demanded.

And then I told her. "Stuff like how you threw a party in your hotel room with Summer and Elise," I said.

Ashley's eyes almost bugged out of her head. *"Are you kidding me?"* she cried.

"Ashley had a party?" Phoebe cut in. "How come I wasn't invited?"

I quickly filled Phoebe in on the whole story. About how Ashley and her friends ordered tons of room service but didn't have any money to pay for it. And how they made a secret deal with the manager to work off the bill so our chaperons, Ms. Clare and Mr. Turnbull, wouldn't find out.

"Oh," Phoebe said.

Ashley dropped down on the sand and buried

her face in her hands. "Mary-Kate, how could you?" she said in a muffled voice.

"I just thought . . ." I began.

What *did* I think? I wondered. How could I ever believe I could trust Dana?

"What am I going to do?" Ashley wailed. "Dana's right. If Mr. Turnbull or Ms. Clare find out, they probably *will* send me home!"

"I'm really sorry," I said in a small voice.

Ashley glanced at me, but she didn't say a word.

"You know what?" Phoebe turned to Ashley. "There's a totally decent chance Dana won't rat on you."

"Yeah," I said quickly. "She's having way too much fun torturing you." *I hope,* I added silently.

Ashley was still quiet. Then she smiled a little. "It's okay, guys," she said. "No big deal. You're probably right."

I gave my sister a giant hug. "So you're not mad at me?" I just wanted to make sure.

Ashley sighed. "Just don't let Dana fool you again," she said. "And no more spilling my secrets to anyone. Got it?"

"Got it," I said, holding up one hand. "Never again. I promise."

"Okay, everyone!" Lani called out. "Back over

here. We're all going to practise surfing with a buddy now." She read some names off a list. "Julia Langstrom and Elise Van Hook. Jeremy Burke and Summer Sorenson. Mary-Kate Burke and Campbell Smith . . ."

I perked up. "Campbell and I are partners?" I whispered to Ashley. "This is great. Now she'll *have* to talk to me."

"Good luck, Mary-Kate," Ashley said as I grabbed my board.

I walked across the hot sand to where Campbell was standing with her board. "Hey," I said extra-cheerfully.

"Hi," Campbell said.

Okay, not overly friendly, but it's a start, I thought.

"So what do you think of the class so far?" I asked.

Campbell shrugged. "It's fine."

All right! I cheered. *We're having a real conversation. Almost.*

"So maybe—" I began.

"Look," Campbell cut in, "I'm sorry, but I don't really feel like talking right now."

My heart sank. "Campbell, you know I'm sorry for what happened back in Hilo. Can't we just start over?" I asked. "We're best friends, right?"

There. It was probably some kind of record. Two apologies in about two minutes. One to my sister and one to my roommate.

Campbell was silent for a minute. Was that a good sign? Was she finally going to forgive me?

"Mary-Kate," Campbell began, "you believed Dana instead of me. You accused me of stealing. A real best friend wouldn't do that."

She stared directly into my eyes. She totally meant what she said. And I didn't realise it until right then, but Campbell wasn't just angry with me. She was really hurt.

"But . . ." My voice trailed off. What else could I say? Campbell was right. Best friends don't turn their backs on each other. And that's exactly what I did.

We paddled our boards out into the water in silence. In fact, we didn't say a word to each other for the next half hour – even when we both wiped out at the same time.

That's when I decided I was going to start Operation: Autograph the second we got back to the hotel.

I had to prove to Campbell that I care about her. That she can trust me again. That I really am her best friend.

Dear Diary,

When I got to my room I threw on a pair of shorts and a tank top over my bathing suit and hurried back down to the lobby with a pen and a piece of hotel stationery.

I was on a mission. I was going to get Jake's autograph for Campbell no matter what it took.

I checked the pool, the gym, the gift shop, the ballroom and the Luau Lounge.

No cat-carrying baseball players.

Finally I peeked into the Coconut Room, one of the fancy restaurants at the resort. It looked like the kind of place someone famous would have lunch.

Score! There was Jake, sitting at a corner table with one of his bodyguards.

I knew the bodyguards had said no autographs. But once they heard my story, I was sure they would let me talk to Jake.

I quietly made my way through the tables in the restaurant. *I'm only a few feet away from him*, I thought excitedly. *I can't believe how easy this—*

"Jake Nakamoto!" a woman cried suddenly. "It's *him!*"

"Uh-oh," I said under my breath.

Loud footsteps sounded behind me. A large group of tourists ran by, waving pens in the air.

They swarmed around Jake's table. "Jake! Jake, can we have your autograph?" one of them shouted. "Look this way, Jake! Say cheese!"

A camera flashed.

One of Jake's bodyguards jumped up from his seat and stood in front of Jake. "Mr. Nakamoto is trying to relax. No autographs," he barked. "And no more pictures, please."

I squeezed through to the front of the crowd. "Excuse me, sir," I said to the bodyguard. He must have been seven feet tall.

The bodyguard glared at me. "What?"

"Well, I know you said Jake isn't signing autographs," I said quickly. "But I have a total emergency. My best friend isn't talking to me. And I just know she'll be my friend again if I get Jake's autograph for her."

"*That's* your emergency?" the bodyguard asked.

I nodded. "So I'm sure you can understand how important this is." I held out my pen and piece of paper.

The man shook his head. "Jake's not signing autographs on this trip."

"But—" I started.

"Sorry, kid," he said. "No exceptions."

"Thanks anyway." I walked away, feeling discouraged. Obviously Jake's bodyguards didn't care that I had lost my best friend.

I glanced back at Jake. Of course he deserved to relax in Hawaii. Everybody did.

But he seemed so nice on all those TV interviews Campbell and I watched together back home. I bet if I told *Jake* my story, he'd understand. He might even give me an autograph.

It was time for Plan B: figure out a way to sneak past those bodyguards!

Dear Diary,

The weirdest thing happened last night. After dinner Summer and Elise invited a bunch of us to watch a DVD in their room. (That's not the weird part. I'll get to it in a second.)

"Okay, is everyone here?" Elise asked.

"Yes!" Summer, Campbell and I said together.

"Present," Phoebe answered.

"Can we just start the movie now?" Dana asked impatiently. "I have an early spa appointment in the morning."

"Wait a sec, Mary-Kate isn't here yet," I pointed out.

Just then the door burst open and Mary-Kate came rushing in. "Sorry I'm late!" she said. "What are we watching?"

"You're just in time," Elise replied, popping in the DVD.

"The movie is called *Return of the Killer Pod People*," Summer announced. "It's based on a true story about aliens."

"Oh, boy," I muttered. All through dinner Summer had been going on and on about aliens.

 She'd heard some weird guy talking in the lobby about that *Inquisitor* article. According to him, groups of fat little green men had been seen invading the beach.

Give me a break.

Mary-Kate squeezed into an empty space next to Campbell.

Then Campbell did something really mean. She got up and sat next to Julia on the other side of the room!

Poor Mary-Kate, I thought. *She didn't deserve that.*

I had an idea. Campbell and I always got along pretty well. Maybe *I* could talk to her.

I got up and walked over to the bowl of popcorn,

which was on a table behind Campbell. "Hi," I whispered as the movie credits flashed onto the screen.

Campbell turned around. "Hey, Ashley. What's up?"

"Look, maybe this is none of my business," I said, keeping my voice low. "But Mary-Kate feels really terrible—"

Campbell looked back at the screen. "I know, but—"

"She made a huge mistake," I said. "You're her best friend, though. And best friends forgive each other, right?"

"Shh!" Dana said. "I can't hear the movie, Ashley."

I really wanted to snap back at Dana. After all, I was in the middle of something important here! But I was a little worried that she might tell my secret if I did. So I kept quiet.

"Ashley, you're blocking our view," Summer complained. "The aliens are flashing messages from their hideout. I can't read them."

"Just think about it," I whispered to Campbell. I sat next to Mary-Kate to watch the movie.

There was a giant cornfield on the screen. A farmer stood in the field, gazing at the night sky. Creepy music filled the room.

Suddenly a big spaceship with flashing coloured lights appeared. The farmer screamed. Then he threw down his pitchfork and started to run.

Elise screamed, too. "He doesn't have a chance! They're going to get him!"

"You can't outrun aliens," Summer said. "That's a total fact."

A huge beam of bright blue light came down from the spaceship and swooped up the farmer.

"They're going to do experiments on him," Summer said. "But not yet. Keep watching."

The scene changed to a deserted beach, where a young couple was taking a romantic walk.

The spaceship appeared again and beamed the woman away.

Summer passed over the bowl of microwave popcorn. "Can you believe that this actually happened?" she whispered.

"Not really," I muttered.

"No, it did," Elise whispered. "I read all about the making of this movie in *Hollywood Gossip* magazine. They interviewed the director, who swears that it's a true story!"

I munched on some popcorn and watched the UFO land in a desert somewhere. Creepy green men with three huge red eyes in their heads emerged and began to search for something. Everywhere they went they left a long trail of yellow slime.

"Gross," Mary-Kate said.

"Ew!" Julia cried.

"Check this part out," Summer said, pointing to the TV. "They're making patterns with those little purple glowing rocks."

Phoebe frowned. "Wait a second, Summer," she said. "Didn't that article you were reading say something about little purple shells . . . ?"

I turned my face away from the screen, trying not to laugh. I hoped Phoebe was just saying that as a joke.

Something outside the window caught my eye. Bright, flashing lights were flickering in the darkness.

Mary-Kate noticed them, too. "What's that?" she said.

Everyone turned to look. The lights kept flashing on and off. They seemed to be getting closer and closer.

Suddenly a huge rush of air blew the curtains straight up into the air.

"Oh, no!" Summer shrieked, dropping the bowl of popcorn. "It's the aliens! They're coming to get us!"

Dear Diary,

Guess what happened next, Diary. Elise started screaming. So did everybody else.

But I kept my cool. I had to see what was out there, though. I jumped up and hurried to the window to get a closer look.

"Ashley, don't!" Elise cried.

"They'll kidnap you and freeze you and stick you in a giant test tube!" Summer added. "Ooh, I can't watch." She buried her head under a pillow.

I peered out the window.

"Take us to your leader!" an eerie-sounding voice called.

"Nooooo!" Elise shrieked.

"Shh!" I said, motioning with my hand.

"Leader . . . leader . . . leader . . ." the voice echoed.

I frowned. Hey, wait a minute. That sounded like . . .

"Jeremy, is that you?" I yelled.

"No," the voice mumbled from the bushes.

I looked closer. Sure enough, Jeremy and Hans were hiding in some flower bushes under the window. They were waving around big flashlights and turning them on and off.

I opened the window wider and leaned out. "You two are *so* dumb!" I shouted.

"Not dumb enough to believe there was an alien spaceship outside your window," Jeremy said. He and Hans cracked up.

My friends gathered around the window.

"Don't make fun of aliens!" Summer burst out. She threw a handful of popcorn at the boys. Hans ducked. But Jeremy caught some popcorn and stuffed it into his mouth.

"Let's just finish the movie," I said.

But no one wanted to watch anymore. Not even Phoebe. They were too busy talking about aliens again.

Diary, I cannot tell you how sick I am of the whole subject. Has everyone gone nuts? Even Mary-Kate was getting into it. Luckily, the next day at lunch we had something else to talk about.

Phoebe, Elise, Summer and I were sitting at a table in the hotel coffee shop. The waitress brought our food, and we all dug in.

"This veggie burger tastes really weird, you

guys," Phoebe said after a few bites.

Phoebe's totally serious about her veggie burgers. She's doing the whole vegetarian thing. She's even got a rating of the diners near  White Oak based on the quality of their veggie burgers. Phoebe slid her plate over to me. "Here, try it."

I picked up the burger and tasted it. "Seems okay to me," I said. "Except it needs more ketchup."

"Try it again," Phoebe urged me.

I took another bite. "You're right," I said, shrugging. "It needs more relish, too."

Phoebe shook her head. "That's not what I meant. I think I tasted *meat* in it. It's supposed to be a *veggie* burger!"

"No way," I told her. "There is no meat in this."

"Let me taste," Elise said, reaching over. She bit into the burger. "Mmm, yummy!"

"Wait, I want to try." Summer grabbed the burger from Elise and took a huge bite. She chewed thoughtfully. "I think they put pineapple in it!"

"Pineapple? Really?" I asked. "Let me taste it again." Summer handed me the burger, and I took another bite.

"Uh, guys? Can I have my lunch back?" Phoebe asked.

I handed Phoebe the bite of burger that was left. "Sorry, Phoebe. Looks like we got a little carried away."

Phoebe sighed. "That's okay. But I could have sworn I tasted meat in there."

I jumped up. "I'll order you fries," I said.

I hurried toward the counter to find the waitress. Sitting there on the last stool was Ms. Clare. My stomach sank when I saw who was right beside her. Dana Woletsky!

And I had a feeling I knew what they were talking about.

I ducked into the phone area around the corner. Luckily, they hadn't seen me.

My heart pounded hard. Was it possible? Had Dana reached a new all-time low? Was she actually trying to have me sent home?

"Are you sure about this, Dana?" I heard Ms. Clare ask.

"It's true. Back in Hilo Ashley Burke had a big party in her hotel room," Dana said.

I gasped. She *was* ratting on me!

"She ran up a huge room-service bill," Dana went on. "Then she had to make a secret deal with the manager of the hotel to pay it off."

I clamped a hand over my mouth. I was doomed. I had to do some damage control – fast!

I ran back to the counter.

Ms. Clare raised her eyebrows. "Ashley, what a coincidence. Dana was just telling me about a little party you had. Would you like to explain?" she asked.

I glanced at Dana. She looked totally smug.

"Well, I *did* have a party," I said. "I guess Summer and Elise and I were so bummed about not being in Wild Hawaii that we wanted to cheer ourselves up."

Okay, so that wasn't exactly true. We were happy to be kicked out of Wild Hawaii. But Ms. Clare didn't have to know that.

"We found out later that the room service wasn't included in our vacation," I went on. "We didn't have the money to pay for what we ordered so we went to the manager and offered to work it off." I looked at the floor. "We were afraid to tell you."

Ms. Clare folded her arms. "Ashley, you should have come to me when it happened," she said. "That would have been the right thing to do."

"I know," I replied. "And I'm really sorry. But we were too embarrassed. We waited on tables and washed dishes and cleaned rooms for days."

Ms. Clare was silent for a minute. Was she going to send me home? I held my breath.

Finally our chaperon smiled and patted my shoulder. "I think you've learned your lesson," she said. "But from now on, no more room service, okay?"

I let out a huge sigh of relief. "Thank you, Ms. Clare!" I exclaimed. "I'll be on my best behaviour for the rest of the trip."

Ms. Clare nodded and turned back to her lunch.

I smiled at Dana, who scowled and stomped off.

Yes! I cheered. Now I could relax and enjoy this awesome vacation!

Dear Diary,

I caught Ashley up on Plan B of Operation: Autograph while we were at the pool this afternoon.

"What does this guy look like again?" Ashley asked.

I took a sip of my pineapple smoothie. "Ashley, how can you be so clueless about one of the most famous baseball players in the world?"

Ashley shrugged. "It's kind of like the time I was talking about clogs and you thought I meant the kind that stop up the drain."

I grinned. "Okay, never mind," I said. "Jake is six two with short black hair and tanned skin. He usually wears a red baseball cap—"

"Sounds like you're describing that guy over there," Ashley broke in.

I followed Ashley's gaze and almost dropped my smoothie. "That's him!"

Jake was settling into a beach chair across the deck. He slipped on a pair of sunglasses and started to read a magazine.

"He's alone. I've got to talk to him," I said. I jumped up from my chair – just as one of his bodyguards walked over and sat down next to him.

I froze in my tracks. "Oh, great." I groaned. "*Now* what do I do?"

"I know!" Ashley snapped her fingers. "You could pretend to be a towel girl and bring Jake some towels. The bodyguard won't stop you if he thinks you're just doing your job."

"Ashley, you are a genius!" I cried.

"You should bring him some sunscreen, too," Ashley suggested.

I nodded. "Jake always uses Sportsun, SPF 15. He even did a commercial for the stuff."

"Go for it!" Ashley cheered.

I ran to the towel hut and grabbed some fresh towels and a bottle of sunscreen. Then I put on my shades and pulled my hair into a ponytail. I didn't want his bodyguard to recognise me from yesterday.

"Wish me luck!" I said to Ashley over my shoulder as I started toward Jake.

She gave me a thumbs-up sign.

I strolled over to Jake's chair. He glanced up and smiled.

"Can I offer you a fresh towel?" I asked. "I also have some Sportsun SPF 15 handy, just in case you need it."

Jake sat up in his chair. "Well, thanks," he said.

Yes! I thought. This was going great. "So, Jake, I was wondering—"

"Thanks, miss." Jake's bodyguard got out of his chair. He grabbed the towels and the sunscreen. "Mr. Nakamoto needs some privacy now."

"It's okay," Jake said to the bodyguard. "What were you going to say?" he asked me.

Ring, ring!

"Excuse me a second," Jake said. He pulled a mobile phone out of his pocket and flipped it open. "Hello?"

"So was there anything else you wanted to ask

Mr. Nakamoto?" the bodyguard asked.

My heart started thudding in my chest. *Just tell him you want Jake to sign a napkin*, I thought. But I was so nervous! I mean, I knew the bodyguard wasn't going to let me stick around for an autograph. "Uh, I wanted to see if he needed a smoothie or something."

"He's all set," the guard replied. "He has a smoothie right here." He pointed to a cup resting on a small table next to Jake's chair.

I racked my brain for some other excuse to hang around.

"What do you mean, the deadline's been moved up?" Jake said into the phone.

"You should probably go now," the bodyguard told me. "Thanks."

I stared helplessly at Jake, but he didn't look like he was getting off the phone anytime soon. There was nothing I could do except leave.

I dragged myself back to my chair. Ashley leaned in. "So? How did it go?" she asked.

"Strike two," I replied.

Ashley looked puzzled. "Huh?"

"That's baseball talk for: I

135

didn't get the autograph this time, either," I explained glumly.

"Oh. Right," Ashley replied. "Does that mean one more strike and you're out?"

I hoped not.

Chapter 4

Monday

Dear Diary,

Okay, now I've moved on to Plan C of Operation: Autograph. I'm going to find out Jake's room number, stand outside his door, and ambush him when he comes out!

I asked for Jake's room number at the front desk, but they wouldn't tell me. So right after Ms. Clare and Mr. Turnbull took us on a glass-bottom boat ride, I walked into the hotel florist. I had an awesome idea.

"May I help you?" the man behind the counter asked.

"I'd like to have a rose delivered to a guest in the resort right away," I said.

The florist nodded. "Very well. What colour?"

"Um, whatever," I said.

The man gave me a puzzled look. "And whom would you like it delivered to?" he asked.

"Jake Nakamoto," I replied.

"What would you like the card to say?" the man asked.

"Card?" I repeated blankly. "Um, I don't need a card."

The florist raised an eyebrow. "One rose, any colour, for Jake Nakamoto," he said. "No card."

"Yup. Thanks!" I said. I paid the bill and walked out.

But I didn't go very far. I hung out in the hallway outside the florist's shop and watched as he boxed up a single pink rose and handed it to a delivery guy.

The guy nodded at something the florist said, then walked out of the store with the box.

Excellent! My plan was working.

The guy was going to deliver that rose to Jake's room. And when he did, I would be right behind him!

We both took the lift to the top floor of the resort and got out. I made sure I stayed far enough behind the delivery guy so he wouldn't notice me.

He walked to the end of the hall and knocked on a door that said Penthouse A. "Flower delivery for Mr. Nakamoto," he called.

The door opened and one of Jake's bodyguards stepped out. As he signed for the flower, a white,

furry cat slipped out into the hall and ran toward me.

Snowball!

I grabbed the cat as she hurried

by me. No one even noticed. The bodyguard closed the door, and the delivery guy stepped back into the lift.

"Purr-fect!" I told Snowball. "The bodyguards will be so grateful I brought you back, they'll have to let me talk to Jake."

Snowball hissed and twisted and jumped out of my arms.

"Snowball, come back!" I begged. "You're my best hope!"

I tried to grab the cat again, but she scurried down the hall.

"Snowball!" I whispered. "Come on, pleeease! Come to Mary-Kate!"

I inched closer and reached out my arms. The cat's green eyes squinted at me.

"Gotcha!" I cried, grabbing her.

I held the cat close to my chest so she couldn't get away.

"Mrwow!" Snowball wriggled back and forth.

"Good kitty, gooood kitty," I said as I speed-walked to Jake's room. I knocked on the door with my elbow. It wasn't easy. Snowball was squirming like crazy.

Okay, this is it, I thought. I was finally going to get to talk to Jake about the autograph!

Suddenly Snowball dug her claws into my arm. "Ow!" I cried.

I loosened my grip, and she jumped to the ground. One second later Jake's bodyguard opened the door.

Snowball ran straight into Jake's room. The

guard barely looked at me before he closed the door.

"Hey, wait a second!" I protested just as the door slammed in my face.

Strike three.

Dear Diary,

After a huge, delicious buffet dinner, Summer, Elise and I decided to take a walk on the beach.

Phoebe wasn't feeling too well. I guess she was still recovering from her non-veggie burger.

And Mary-Kate was just too bummed to come with us. I feel really bad for her. She's been trying so hard to get that autograph for Campbell. I wish Campbell could see that Mary-Kate really is a great friend.

"Just look at that sky!" Summer breathed, tilting her head back.

I gazed up at the swirls of pink, purple and blue

that painted the air. "It's beautiful," I agreed.

Then something weird happened. Some of the colors started blinking! Red, green, yellow . . . What was going on?

The lights got lower and lower until they were flashing just above the palm trees.

"That's really strange," I told my friends.

"They look just like those lights from the UFO in that movie we watched," Elise said slowly.

Summer gasped. "The killer pod people are returning," she breathed. "It's really happening!"

"Get real, Summer," I said. "There's no such thing as—"

Summer and Elise started running down the beach toward the lights.

"Come on, Ashley!" Summer yelled. "We have to see where they went!"

We do? I thought, taking off after my friends. I had to admit, I was a little curious. We ran all the way to the other side of the resort.

"We lost them!" Summer cried when we reached a rose garden. She sounded really disappointed. "Where did the lights go?"

"It seemed like they were coming from right here," Elise said.

A bush rustled nearby.

Elise and Summer grabbed each other's arm in fright.

"Who's there?" I asked, a little nervous.

I inched toward the bush. "Hello?" I asked, pushing some leaves aside. I saw a lock of long, curly brown hair – Phoebe's hair.

"Guys, relax," I told Summer and Elise. "It's just Phoebe."

But why was she hiding in the bushes? And why wasn't she answering me? I tapped her on the shoulder. "Phoebe? You okay?"

Phoebe gasped. When she saw that it was me, she seemed to relax a little. "Oh . . . hi," she said. "Um, what's up?"

"Maybe I should ask *you* that," I replied. "What are you doing hiding in the rosebushes?"

"Oh . . . um . . . I'm not hiding. I just wanted to . . . get a closer look at this type of flower." She emerged from the bushes, holding her video camera and backpack. "They're pretty, right?"

"Sure," I said. Then I noticed the scratches. Red X marks covered both her arms. "Phoebe, you're bleeding. Look!"

"Oh . . . yeah," she said, not really concerned.

"From the thorns on the roses, I guess. I'm okay."

Summer and Elise ran up to her.

"Did you just see the UFO?" Summer demanded. "We saw the lights from the other side of the resort."

"UFO?" Phoebe repeated. She laughed nervously. "Uh, nope. No UFOs around here!"

"See, I told you," I said to Summer and Elise. But something weird was going on with Phoebe. She seemed so . . . distracted. I mean, how could she not notice those scratches?

"Whatever," Summer replied. She didn't look convinced, though.

"What are you taping?" I asked Phoebe. I peeked at the little screen on the video camera. "And I thought you said you were sick."

Phoebe quickly pulled the camera away from me. "This video is top secret!" she said. "No one can see it but me." She stuffed the camera into her backpack.

Whoa! I thought. "Sorry," I said. "I didn't mean to—"

"Look, I have to go," Phoebe said, standing up. "I'll see you guys later, okay? Bye." She took off back toward the beach.

"Hmmm. Was Phoebe acting really strange just

now or what?" I asked Summer and Elise.

"Totally weird," Summer replied. "And I bet I know why."

She picked up a small blue metal tube from the ground. "This fell out of Phoebe's backpack when she put the camera in it."

"What is it?" Elise asked.

I peered closer. "I bet that's just a broken pen or something."

"That *National Inquisitor* article said that they found scraps of blue metal just like this at the scene of the other alien sighting," Summer pointed out. "They think it was part of the spaceship."

Elise gasped. "No way!"

"There's only one explanation," Summer continued. "A UFO was here. And Phoebe saw it!"

Chapter 5

Tuesday

Dear Diary,

Tonight we had a luau on the beach. That's a special kind of Hawaiian barbecue where you roast a pig over an open fire, which is dug into the ground.

We're talking about a whole pig with an apple in its mouth!

Jeremy and Grant were crawling around the beach on all fours and squealing, "Oink, oink!" I swear, they are such babies! Luckily, Ms. Clare made them stop.

Campbell was sitting with Julia, of course. They were eating fresh pineapple slices and giggling about something.

I sat across the fire from them, feeling pretty awful. I still hadn't got Jake's autograph, and Campbell wasn't showing any signs of coming around.

Ashley sat down next to me and handed me a coconut shell cup filled with mango juice. "So how is Operation: Autograph going?" she asked.

I told Ashley all about the Snowball episode. "I

have no idea what to do next," I sighed. "I haven't spotted Jake all day. And Campbell is still ignoring me."

"Well, you've done all you could to make up with her," Ashley said. "Maybe you should just forget about the whole autograph thing and enjoy yourself."

"But she's my best friend, Ashley. What would you do if Phoebe all of a sudden hated you? Wouldn't you try everything to get her to *stop* hating you?"

"Okay, okay," Ashley said. "You've got a point." She paused. "You know what, Mary-Kate? Maybe you could show Campbell you're sorry by doing something nice for her. Not something huge, like getting Jake's autograph. Something small. Why don't you send over her favourite ice cream?"

"Well, I'll try it," I said. "But I'm still going to get that autograph if it's the last thing I do." I waved to a nearby waiter. He smiled and came over.

"Can you please send that girl with the blue T-shirt a bowl of chocolate fudge ice cream?" I pointed across the bonfire at Campbell.

"No problem, miss," the waiter said.

"Just make sure she knows it's from me, okay?" I added.

The waiter nodded. As he
turned to leave, he almost crashed
into Phoebe, who was running by.

"*There* she is!" Ashley said,
jumping up. "I have to go catch
Phoebe. She's been acting kind of
weird lately."

"What's wrong with her?" I asked.

"I have no clue," Ashley answered. "But I'm
going to find out!" She tore off after Phoebe.

I watched as the waiter came back with the ice
cream and handed it to Campbell. He said something and pointed to me. Campbell shook her head
and said something back to the waiter. He hesitated,
then walked over to me.

"I'm sorry, miss. She says she doesn't want it," he
told me. "Would you like to eat it instead?"

"No, thanks," I replied. I felt totally embarrassed.
And now I was a little angry, too.

I'd tried and tried to make up with Campbell.
But she obviously didn't care whether we'd ever be
best friends again.

Well, if that's the way she wants it, I thought, *then
that's fine with me.*

From now on I was going to forget about trying
to win back Campbell!

Dear Diary,

I am really getting worried about Phoebe. I'm sure she didn't see a UFO, but something is definitely up.

I tried to talk to her after the luau tonight. I found her in one of the elaborate hotel gardens, looking through a big telescope.

"Hey, Phoebe," I said. I pointed to the stuffed backpack she had slung over a shoulder. "Going somewhere?" I joked.

Phoebe straightened up so fast that she almost banged her head on the telescope. "Oh, um, hi, Ashley. I'm not going anywhere. Why would you think I was going somewhere?" she said really fast.

"It was just a joke," I replied. "Anyway, what are you looking at?" I asked, gesturing to the telescope.

"Just the stars," Phoebe replied.

"Phoebe, there are no stars yet," I pointed out. "It's still daylight."

Phoebe shifted nervously. She glanced at the telescope, then at me.

We didn't say anything for a couple of minutes. I couldn't help staring at the scratches on her arms.

Phoebe noticed. "Oh, don't worry about those. They don't hurt. Really."

I don't know why, Diary, but our conversation seemed very, very tense. I decided to break the ice with one of Phoebe's favourite subjects – poetry.

"So, there's a special Hawaiian poetry reading on the beach tonight," I said. "Do you want to go?"

I figured there was no way she would refuse. Phoebe loved poetry so much she even decorated her half of our dorm room with posters of famous poets!

Phoebe shook her head. "Sorry, but no, thanks. I don't feel like listening to poetry."

Phoebe was turning down a night of poetry? "Phoebe, are you sure nothing is bothering you?" I asked. "You've been acting kind of—"

But Phoebe wasn't listening. She was bending over the telescope. She gasped suddenly. "They're back! I have to get down there right now!"

I tried to look over her shoulder, but I couldn't see what she was talking about. "Who's back?" I asked.

"Nobody," Phoebe said. "I'll see you later, okay?"

"What's going on? Phoebe, wait!" I called after her. But she didn't stop.

I looked through the telescope. It was pointed at a restaurant in the rose garden. Workers were loading boxes off a truck and carrying them into the building. What was the big deal?

Help, Diary! My friend has definitely turned into a total space case!

Chapter 6

Wednesday

Dear Diary,

Six A.M. is way too early to be awake. But that's what time I was up this morning.

It was Ashley's fault, actually. She woke me up by talking in her sleep. Something about telescopes and coloured lights.

And now I can't fall back to sleep. So here I am, looking at the surf and writing in you.

I stared out of the window. It was so pretty outside. The sun was just coming up and the sky was streaked with pink and gold. Palm trees swayed in the breeze. A group of seagulls swooped through the air.

Then I spotted a tall man in a red baseball cap jogging on the beach. I rubbed my eyes. No way! It was Jake Nakamoto – and he was alone!

What should I do? I know I said I was going to forget about Campbell. But maybe, just maybe I overreacted. And here was Jake – right in front of me! It was too easy. I had to try to get his autograph.

I slipped on my sneakers, grabbed a pen and paper, and ran out of the room.

Three minutes later I was tearing down the beach. I could see Jake not that far ahead. He wasn't wearing any shoes, and he was jogging on the wet sand where the waves rolled onto the shore.

The morning air was damp and chilly, but I was already working up a sweat. I was sprinting at full speed, trying to catch up. But I couldn't. "Jake! Hey, Jake!" I yelled.

He didn't seem to hear me. He just kept jogging. I tried to keep going, too, but finally I had to give up. Jake was just too fast. I stopped and clutched my side, breathing hard.

Then I saw two other joggers stretching at the entrance to the beach. I could hear them laughing and talking.

Julia. And Campbell.

I felt a pang. Normally I would go over to Campbell and tell her how I tried to outrun Jake Nakamoto. But hey, she'd probably just ignore me again, right?

I just wish I didn't feel so lonely without her.

Surf, Sand, and Secrets

Dear Diary,

I decided that there had to be a log-ical explanation for Phoebe's weird behaviour. I just didn't know what it was yet.

I hoped that after this morning's hula-dancing class on the beach, I'd have a clear mind and would be able to figure it out. Our instructor was this hunky guy named Konane.

"I am *not* getting in a grass skirt and waving my arms around," Jeremy complained.

"Hula dancing isn't just for women," Konane told him. "In fact, some of the greatest hula dancers in our country have been men."

"Yeah, Jeremy," Hans teased, shaking his hips back and forth. "You'd look sooo cute with flowers in your hair!"

Konane turned to Hans. "Why don't you go first?"

Hans scowled as Konane showed him a couple of steps.

I looked around to find Phoebe. She was sitting away from the group and drawing something in a notebook.

I leaned over to Elise, Summer, and Mary-Kate.

"Phoebe has been totally out of it the last two days," I whispered.

"What do you mean?" Mary-Kate asked, stifling a yawn. She had got up really early this morning for some reason.

I told Mary-Kate about what happened on Monday, when Summer and Elise thought they saw a UFO and we found Phoebe with a video camera instead. Then I told all three of them about Phoebe and the telescope.

Summer's eyes grew enormous. "I know what Phoebe was trying to find through the telescope!"

"What?" Elise, Mary-Kate and I asked at the same time.

"The spaceship!" Summer said.

Here we go again, I thought.

"We have proof that Phoebe saw the UFO on Monday," Summer went on. "The piece of blue metal, remember?"

This alien stuff was really getting out of hand. "You mean the broken pen?" I asked.

Summer ignored me. "The aliens had no choice but to take over Phoebe's brain after she saw them. It's perfectly logical."

"Oh, right." Mary-Kate giggled. "That's perfectly logical."

"I'm serious!" Summer said. "I read about it on the AlienEncounters website. When your mind is taken over by aliens, you start acting jumpy and out of it and not like yourself."

If anyone's brain had been taken over, it was Summer's. On the other hand, she was always acting kind of spacey.

I glanced at Phoebe. She certainly wasn't acting like herself these days. But I was sure there was another reason. And I was going to find out what it was.

"I'll be right back, guys," I said. I walked over to Phoebe, who was now scribbling like mad in a notebook.

"Hey, Phoebe," I said, plopping down next to her huge backpack. "You're still carrying this around? What's in here?"

Phoebe's head shot up. "Why do you keep asking me that?" she said kind of nervously. "Anyway, what's up?"

"Oh, I just came over to say hi," I replied. I glanced at her open book. There were drawings of strange disk-shaped things all over the page. Things that looked just like . . . UFOs.

155

No. Not UFOs, I reminded myself. Boy, Summer and Elise must have really got to me.

Phoebe saw me peeking and slammed her book shut. "Excuse me," she mumbled, jumping to her feet. "I've got to go."

"But you haven't even had a chance to hula yet," I pointed out. "I thought you said you couldn't wait to hula dance."

"I don't care. I'm too busy right now," Phoebe said. "See you later." She gathered her stuff and hurried away.

I sighed and rejoined the others. As I waited for my turn to hula, I made a mental list of all the weird stuff going on with Phoebe lately:

First she freaked out over a veggie burger.

Then there were the strange lights.

Then we found Phoebe hiding in the bushes.

Then she didn't notice the scratches on her arms.

Then there was the telescope incident.

Then there was the huge backpack she's been carrying everywhere.

Then she said no to a poetry reading.

Then she skipped out on hula lessons, which she'd been really looking forward to.

And now she was drawing UFOs in her notebook – or whatever they were.

Wow, that was a lot of weird stuff. No wonder Elise and Summer thought Phoebe had been taken over by space creatures.

The question was: how was I ever going to bring "Alien Phoebe" back to earth?

Chapter 7

Thursday

Dear Diary,

Today I am going to find out for sure what's going on with Phoebe.

Summer and Elise are now officially alien-obsessed, and Mary-Kate is still chasing after Jake. So that means it's up to me.

Phoebe didn't show up at lunch. I ordered a take-out veggie burger for her and went straight to her room.

I knocked on the door. No answer.

I was about to turn away, when I heard papers shuffling inside the room.

I knocked again, louder this time. "Phoebe?" I called. "It's me, Ashley! Can I come in?"

"I'm really busy," Phoebe said through the door.

"But I need to talk to you!" I insisted. "It's important."

I heard Phoebe sigh. She unlocked the door and swung it open.

I gasped. Phoebe was dressed in white Capri pants, white platform shoes and a 4-You T-shirt. Totally *not* her style!

"What's the matter?" she asked.

"Those clothes," I said. "They're so . . . not you!"

Phoebe glanced over her shoulder. "Yeah, well, I'm kind of in the middle of something right now. Can we talk later?"

I stood there stunned. Phoebe wearing non-vintage clothes was almost too much for me to process.

"Okay, then," Phoebe said when I didn't answer. "Bye!" She took the veggie burger from me and closed the door.

That was so rude! Now I knew something was *really* wrong. Phoebe's, like, the sweetest person on the planet. In this galaxy, anyway.

I had to talk to Mary-Kate. Right *now.*

But I couldn't find my sister anywhere. Instead, I ran into Summer and Elise in the hotel lobby. I told them all about my encounter with Phoebe.

"See?" Summer exclaimed. "Her mind has definitely been taken over by aliens. The new clothes are even more proof!"

That idea was so dumb, it wasn't even worth arguing about. But I didn't have any other explanation for the new Phoebe.

"Come on," Summer said. She grabbed my hand and Elise's hand, too. "I want to show you something."

Summer dragged us over to one of the hotel computers in the Internet Cafe. She logged on and punched in a website address.

159

The screen turned black. Then a weird creature popped onto the screen. It had one eye in the centre of its huge forehead like an octopus and an antenna sticking out of its head.

"This is the AlienEncounters website I told you about," Summer explained.

A menu popped up. Summer pointed to the last item on the menu. It said: HAS A LOVED ONE'S MIND BEEN TAKEN OVER BY ALIENS? CLICK HERE.

"That's what we want," she said excitedly and clicked on the text. A new web page popped up on the screen.

"Look!" Summer said. "It says here that the first sign that someone's mind has been taken over by aliens is when 'the person displays uncharacteristic or unusual behaviour.'"

"The new clothes!" Elise cried.

"Among other things," I added glumly.

"'Two. He/she avoids contact with friends and family,'" Summer read aloud.

"Phoebe's been avoiding me for days." I sighed.

"'Three. He/she acts nervous, vague or skittish.'"

I groaned. "Go on."

"'Four,'" Summer said. "'He/she becomes obsessed with the night sky, stargazing and other similar activities.'"

"The telescope," Elise pointed out.

I looked away from the computer screen. It was true. The website described Phoebe perfectly. But aliens weren't real. It couldn't be possible.

"*Now* do you believe me?" Summer asked.

Like I said, there was no use arguing with Summer. She was just too far gone on the whole alien question. But I had to get back to the point. Phoebe needed our help.

"Say I did believe you – and I'm not saying I do," I told Summer. "What could we do for her?"

Summer scrolled down the page on the computer. "Here it is. A section about how to help someone whose mind has been taken over by aliens," she reported.

"'The person has to wear a special metal hat and stand in front of a big mirror,'" Elise read over Summer's shoulder. She frowned. "What's that supposed to do?"

"Duh. The metal blocks the alien transmissions to Phoebe's brain," Summer said. "And then you have to chant a bunch of special words," she added. "I'll print them out for you."

"We have to do this, Ashley," Elise said urgently. "We have to bring Phoebe back to us!"

This was all too bizarre. "Um, guys," I began. "I don't think—"

"You should do it, Ashley," Elise broke in. "You're Phoebe's roommate. You know her best. She trusts you."

Summer handed me the printout. "May the Force be with you," she said.

I can't believe this, I thought. But I had to try *something.* At this point the anti-brainwashing plan was beginning to look good.

Dear Diary,

Has everyone on this trip gone crazy?

It's bad enough that Campbell will probably never speak to me again. But now some of our friends are insisting there are aliens here in Hawaii.

At first the whole idea was kind of funny. But now it's getting serious.

Ashley just told me that Summer and Elise want her to get Phoebe to wear some weird hat and stand in front of a mirror, because Phoebe's mind has been taken over by aliens.

Ashley thinks that's pretty crazy. But she figures it's an excuse to try and reach Phoebe again.

I guess I must be going crazy, too. Because Ashley just asked me to help her do it – and I said yes!

Chapter 8

Friday

Dear Diary,

I took the night off from Operation: Autograph to help Ashley with Operation: Save Phoebe from Aliens.  Jake didn't seem to be around the hotel much anyway. It seemed almost as if he'd disappeared. Maybe he's just trying to avoid autograph-hungry fans (like me).

Or *maybe* he was abducted by those aliens. (Ha-ha!)

Ashley and I sat on my bed and tried to brainstorm the perfect plan. I'm a real pro at plans now.

"Okay, so we have to get Phoebe to wear a metal hat and stand in front of a mirror," Ashley explained.

I leaned back on my pillow. "Sounds like we're going to have to trick her."

"Hmmm," Ashley said, tapping a finger against her lip. "Phoebe isn't easy to trick. She's so logical. Well, usually."

"I know!" I cried. "You said she's into trendy clothes these days, right?"

Ashley shrugged. "So?"

"So we'll make a special hat for her as a present and tell her it's the cool thing to wear. You know, to go with her new look."

"Okay," Ashley said slowly. "But then we'll all need hats!"

I nodded. "No problem. We'll make Phoebe try hers on in front of the bathroom mirror. And while she's standing there, you can try to talk to her again."

"That's totally brilliant!" Ashley exclaimed.

"Thanks," I said. "Let's just hope it's brilliant enough to work."

"Um, Mary-Kate?" Ashley asked. "There's just one thing."

"What's that?" I said.

"Where do we get metal hats?"

I sighed. It's hard to be brilliant *all* the time. But I'd come up with something to help Ashley.

And Alien Phoebe.

Dear Diary,

So there we were, standing in front of Phoebe's door the next morning. But Mary-Kate wasn't the only one with me. Summer and Elise decided to join us.

"We had to come," Summer said. "What if the

aliens showed up? You would totally need our help."

"All right," I replied. "But don't say anything. I want to do all the talking." I didn't want Summer saying anything about aliens to Phoebe.

We all looked pretty weird, wearing those metal hats. We'd made them out of baseball caps, aluminum foil, wire and old soda cans. But we had to wear them if this plan was going to work.

"This is going to be sooo exciting," Summer said.

"Let's just hope it works," I muttered. "Or we may lose Phoebe for good."

Mary-Kate gave me a thumbs-up. "All systems are go," she said.

I took a deep breath and knocked on Phoebe's door again.

"Who is it?" Phoebe called.

"It's Ashley and Mary-Kate," I said. "And Summer and Elise."

The door opened. This time Phoebe was dressed in denim shorts, a black T-shirt with a blue rhinestone star on it, and a brand-new pair of platform sneakers.

I plastered a huge smile on my face. "Hi, Phoebe! Guess what? We brought you a present." I held out the extra hat we'd made.

Phoebe glanced at me and then at the rest of us.

"That's really nice, guys," she said. "Could you give it to me later?" She started to close the door.

Mary-Kate stepped in front of me and stuck her foot in the door. "But we really want you to have it now," she said sweetly. "It's the latest fashion thing. You know, a fad. It could go out of style before you wear it."

Phoebe hesitated. Then she opened the door wider and let us in. "Okay. But you can only hang out for a second."

We all quickly walked into the room. A bunch of notebooks were spread out on Phoebe's bed. She quickly scooped them up and shoved them into a drawer.

Mary-Kate and I exchanged a look. I knew we were wondering the same thing. What was in those notebooks?

Phoebe stuffed her hands into her pockets. "So what did you bring me?" she asked.

Summer grabbed the hat from me and placed it on Phoebe's head. "Ta-da!" she said brightly.

"Uh . . . what's this?" Phoebe asked.

"The latest in Hawaiian headwear!" I replied. "You know, to go with your, um, new look."

"Well, okay." Phoebe shrugged. "Thanks."

"You've got to see how great it looks!" Mary-

Kate insisted. She started pushing Phoebe towards the bathroom. The entire wall above the sink was covered with a mirror. Summer reached into her beach bag and whipped out a piece of paper.

"Mirabilis yokum sageonis filatis. Mirabilis yokum sageonis filatis . . ." Summer began.

Elise joined in.

I groaned. This was exactly why I didn't want Summer to speak! How was I supposed to get Phoebe to listen to me now?

Phoebe turned and stared at me in total confusion. "Ashley, what's going on?"

"It's a special good-luck chant for your new hat!" Mary-Kate improvised.

"Mirabilis yokum sageonis filatis. Mirabilis yokum sageonis filatis . . ." Summer and Elise kept chanting.

Phoebe shook her head. "You guys are acting really weird," she said. "You're starting to freak me out!"

Mary-Kate motioned for me to hurry up. "Um, look, Phoebe, we have to talk to you," I said quickly. "It's for your own good."

Phoebe yanked off the hat. "Look, I don't know what's going on here," she said, "but I have important things to do. I'm on a deadline."

"We had to do all this stuff," Mary-Kate said. "We couldn't reach you any other way."

"Reach me?" Phoebe demanded. "What are you talking about?"

"Your mind has been taken over by aliens!" Summer blurted out.

Phoebe gaped at all of us. "What?" she said.

"Well, that's just it, Phoebe," I began. "Some people think" – I glanced at Summer and Elise – "that aliens may have taken over your brain. But—"

Phoebe whirled around again so fast that the hat slid off her head. Summer and Elise stopped chanting.

"Are you all nuts?" she cried.

"Not me!" I said quickly. "This whole thing was Summer's idea. And even though I don't believe—"

"I really don't have time for this," Phoebe said. "Everybody out!" She started pushing all four of us towards the door. "Go chase some spaceships or something."

"Denial," Summer said to me under her breath. "It's another one of the signs."

"I'll talk to you later, after you've got your own

brains back," Phoebe said. "And after I finish what I'm working on."

Before the door slammed behind us, I looked over Phoebe's shoulder. Her computer screen was glowing green in the darkened room. And there was a half-eaten veggie burger on her desk.

For some reason I got a chill. What was Phoebe doing? What could be so important?

"Goodbye," Phoebe called through the door. "And have a nice trip to Mars."

The four of us started slowly back down the hall, feeling totally discouraged. And that's when we saw it.

A trail of tiny purple shells . . .

Chapter 9

Saturday

Dear Diary,

It's almost bedtime. I'm sitting on the terrace outside our hotel room. Ashley is watching the Sci Fi Channel with Summer and Elise. Sort of.

They're all still bummed about the Phoebe situation. Summer and Elise are trying to figure out the deal with the trail of shells.

I keep telling them that those shells are all over the resort, but they keep insisting that the aliens put them there.

Ashley was right. No more space movies for them!

I really wish I could help Ashley brainstorm a way to deal with Phoebe. But I have my own thinking to do. Did I really want to come up with another plan to get Jake's autograph for Campbell? Even though I was angry with her, the answer was yes.

Watching the waves and the palm trees helps me think. Oh, and the caramel-swirl ice cream cone I got downstairs helps, too.

I'm thinking.

I'm still thinking.

Ugh! I can't come up with anything!

I feel so helpless. I have to admit I really miss Campbell. If she never talks to me again, who am I going to sneak out of the dorm with late at night to grab a slice of pizza from the kitchen? Who am I going to talk about baseball with? And who else but Campbell would want to spend an entire Saturday at the movie theatre with me watching four movies in a row?

I guess those fun times are over. I'll probably have to get a new roommate next fall, too.

I know it's not like me to give up. But after all this, I don't know what else to do. I've tried everything!

It's sad, but I just have to face it. Campbell and I will never be friends again.

Dear Diary,

You'll never guess what happened. Phoebe ran up and grabbed me by the arm right after wave-running class. She was wearing a Hawaiian-print mini dress.

"We have something super-important to do," Phoebe whispered.

"Can I change into my clothes first?" I asked, pointing to the bathing suit I was wearing.

Phoebe shook her head. "There's no time."

"Okay," I said. Was this about what Phoebe had been working on?

"In an hour the hotel's rose garden restaurant starts serving lunch," Phoebe explained. "If we sneak into the kitchen now, we can catch them!"

"Catch who?" I asked. I was really beginning to worry now. And why were we going to the rose garden? "Phoebe, does this have anything to do with" – I couldn't believe I was about to say it – "aliens?"

"There's no time to explain the whole thing now," Phoebe said, "but the story is out of this world. It's so huge I might even sell it to a real newspaper!" Phoebe reached into her backpack and whipped out her video camera. "We're going to get the whole thing on tape."

A story about aliens . . . in a kitchen? Ooookay. I decided just to play along. Anything to help my roommate – and find out once and for all what was going on.

We sneaked down the hall to the kitchen and peeked inside.

The kitchen was crawling with men and women in checked trousers who were chopping vegetables and washing pots and pans.

"How are we going to get in there without anyone seeing us?" I whispered.

Phoebe held up her hand. "I have a plan. Just wait."

We waited and waited. Then all of a sudden Phoebe whispered, "Now! We're going in!"

She opened the doors, ducked down, and raced towards a chopping table that had a dust ruffle hanging over the sides. I ran in behind her, and we both dropped under the table.

My heart was racing. I took a few deep breaths and tried to calm down. "Now what?" I whispered. "What, um . . . are we looking for?"

"Now we wait," Phoebe replied, turning on the video camera.

This was making me a little nervous. What if Ms. Clare found out I was staking out the kitchen in search of little green men? She'd send me home for sure!

I leaned back on the floor. "Ewww!" I cried softly as my hand touched something squishy. It was an ancient-looking onion ring.

ANCIENT-LOOKING ONION RING

"Oh, gross," I said, wiping my hand against my bathing suit.

All of a sudden the kitchen doors swung open. A man wearing a tall white chef's hat walked in. Another man was right behind him.

"Now, about that burger recipe," the chef said to the man.

I took a look at the man's face. My eyes widened in surprise.

"Hey!" I whispered. "That's Jake Nakamoto, the famous baseball player."

"What's he doing in here?" Phoebe wondered.

"I've been thinking about it," Jake replied, "and I think we should add even more meat to the veggie burgers."

I was totally confused. "Why would Jake tell the chef to put meat in the veggie burgers?" I whispered.

Phoebe shrugged. "I have no idea," she said. "But with luck we're about to find out."

"I have a conference call in five minutes," Jake went on. "Why don't we finish discussing this later?"

"Very good, sir," the chef replied.

Jake said good-bye and left.

"This is big," Phoebe muttered. "This is really big!" She yanked on my hand. "Let's go!"

"Where are we going now?" I asked.

"Duh!" Phoebe announced. "We're going to follow Jake!"

Dear Diary,

Chapter 10

Saturday contd.

Phoebe and I rushed out of the kitchen. Along the way I grabbed a chef's apron and tied it over my  bathing suit. It had food stains all over it, but this wasn't exactly the time to be picky.

We could see Jake hurrying down the hall. He was wearing his shades, and he had his baseball cap low over his forehead.

Wait until Mary-Kate hears about this! I thought.

"I can't believe Jake Nakamoto is involved in this scam," Phoebe said.

"Scam?" I asked blankly.

But Phoebe was pulling me along at warp speed. "There he goes!" she cried.

Jake turned down the hall and disappeared from view.

Phoebe held up her video camera. "We have to stay with him," she insisted.

"Uh, Phoebe, is Jake an . . . alien?" I asked. Is that what Phoebe was thinking? Was she filming a segment for some TV unreality show?

Phoebe didn't answer. We were both running too fast after Jake. We passed Elise and Summer coming out of one of the gift shops. They were carrying a bunch of magazines.

"Ashley, where are you going?" Elise asked.

"And what are you *wearing*?" Summer cried. "Gross."

"No time now. Talk to you later!" I called.

"We'd better make a new hat for Ashley, too," I heard Elise say as I raced by.

We turned the corner. Jake was only about ten feet down the hall.

"Jake, stop!" Phoebe yelled.

Jake turned around. He glanced at Phoebe's video camera, then hurried to the lift and pressed the button about ten times.

Phoebe and I sprinted like crazy to catch up. We were almost there when the lift doors opened. "Sorry, girls. No time for autographs right now," Jake said as he stepped in.

"Wait, Mr. Nakamoto!" Phoebe said. "We need to talk to you. Take us with you."

I looked at Phoebe in alarm. "Take us where?" I said.

But just then the lift doors closed in our faces.

"Oh, man!" Phoebe said, leaning back against the

wall. "We just blew our big chance."

Our big chance for what? A ride in an alien spaceship?

Poor Phoebe was in worse shape than I thought.

Dear Diary,

You will never, ever believe what happened to me today. I was in the lift going to my room when the doors opened and a man jumped in.

"That was close," he muttered and pressed Penthouse.

My mouth dropped open. I blinked a few times to make sure I wasn't seeing things.

Standing next to me, without a single bodyguard, was Jake Nakamoto!

I took a deep breath. "H-hi," I said.

Jake nodded at me. "Hi."

Jake Nakamoto just said hi to me! I silently screamed. *Okay, Mary-Kate, get a grip.*

"Um, I think you're a great baseball player," I went on.

Jake smiled. "Well, thanks."

"That was an awesome grand slam you hit in Game Three of the playoffs last year," I told him.

"Yeah, that was one of my favourites, too," Jake said. "Wish I'd hit another one this season."

I can't believe we're having a real conversation, I said to myself. Now was the perfect time to ask him for an autograph.

"Jake, can you please do me a really big favour?" I said.

Jake raised an eyebrow. "What's that?" he replied.

"My best friend – well, my ex best friend – is your number one fan," I explained. "Even bigger than me. She actually knows all your batting averages from the time you started out in the minor leagues."

"Really?" Jake said. He sounded surprised. And a little flattered, I think.

"Well, Campbell – that's my friend's name – she and I had a big fight," I went on. "It was all my fault, and now she won't speak to me. But if I got your autograph for her, I'm sure she'd forgive me."

The lift doors opened at the top floor. He stepped out.

Oh, no! I thought. *Is it happening again? Is he just going to disappear?*

Jake turned back and held open the door. "Okay," he said. "I'll give you an autograph for your friend. But let's keep it just between us, okay?"

"Oh, thank you, thank you, Jake!" I gushed, reaching into my pocket for a pen and paper.

Oh, no. I left them in my room! "Uh, do you have any paper?" I asked hopefully.

Jake shook his head. "Listen, I'm really late for a conference call," he said. "But I'll tell you what. Why don't you meet me at Diamond Point tomorrow morning – say, six A.M. – and I'll give you that autograph?"

Six? Ugh. But hey, at this point I'd get up at three! I nodded eagerly.

"I know that's kind of early, but my morning jog is the only time I have to myself. And don't worry, one of my bodyguards does keep a watch on the beach with binoculars, so you'll be safe."

"No problem," I said. " I'll be there!"

How about that, Diary? All I needed was one tiny miracle. And I finally got it!

Chapter 11

Sunday

Dear Diary,

This journalism stuff is hard work. Phoebe and I woke up at six this morning. Mary-Kate told me that she saw Jake jogging by himself early the other day so I thought, with any luck, we might catch him today.

Mary-Kate wasn't in her bed. She had left me a note that said "Went for a walk."

I feel as if I haven't seen Mary-Kate in forever. Phoebe and I were super-busy trying to track down Jake yesterday. But she still refuses to tell me exactly what's going on.

Either Phoebe thinks Jake is an alien or she thinks he's trying to meet up with aliens. She keeps muttering something about a "plan."

I haven't figured it out yet. But I'm going to stick really close to Phoebe so I can keep an eye on her.

"Ashley, open up!" Phoebe called from the hallway, pounding on the door.

I rolled out of bed to let her in. She was dressed in vintage clam-diggers and an old khaki shirt. Was "Normal Phoebe" back? Well, normal for *her*, anyway!

"Ready to go?" she asked.

"Uh-huh." I nodded. We walked down to the beach. The air was cool and salty-smelling. The

sand was damp and cov- ered with broken shells and seaweed.

"Let's try this way," I suggested, pointing left. "That's the direction my sister said Jake ran the other day."

"Okay," Phoebe agreed. She pulled her video camera out of her backpack. "I'm all set."

We trudged along the beach for about a mile or so. Finally I saw a man wearing a baseball cap, jogging toward Diamond Point. Bingo!

"We've got him now!" Phoebe cried. "Let's go!"

Dear Diary,

How cool am I? I had a secret meeting with a famous baseball player this morning. Jake Nakamoto is the best!

"Hey," he called as he jogged over to me.

"Hi!" I said, smiling. "Thanks again for meeting me here."

"My pleasure." Jake leaned against a rock. "When you told me about your friend, I realised something. I've been so wrapped up in business lately, I've forgotten to take time out for the thing I love the most. Talking to my fans!"

"Well, I'm sure glad you took the time out to talk to me!" I exclaimed.

Jake grinned. "So what do you want me to sign?" I reached down to pull a piece of paper from my backpack. That's when I saw two girls running toward us like crazy.

Oh, no! I thought.

Then I looked closer. It was Ashley and Phoebe!

What are they doing here? I wondered.

"Mr. Nakamoto!" Phoebe yelled. "We have a few questions for you!"

Jake shook his head. "You two again," he said. "You were chasing me yesterday. What do you want? Autographs?"

Phoebe pointed the video camera right at his face. "We're reporters," she said breathlessly. "What were you doing in the hotel kitchen yesterday morning?"

Ashley looked a little nervous. "Um, Phoebe," she said. "I don't think this is such a good idea."

"What are you talking about?" Jake asked.

"Don't deny it, mister. We know the truth." Phoebe zoomed the video camera lens closer to his face.

Jake held his hands up in front of his face. Then he turned to me with a frown. "Sorry, Mary-Kate. I can't do this right now. It's getting out of hand." He started running back towards the hotel.

"You can run if you want, Mr. Nakamoto!" Phoebe called after him. "But the truth will come out!"

Ashley put an arm around Phoebe's shoulders. "Phoebe, everything's going to be okay," she said. "Just take it easy, all right?"

Then she turned to me. "Mary-Kate, what are you doing here?" she asked.

"Me? What about *you*?" I dropped to the sand, totally bummed. "I was about to get Jake's autograph," I said miserably. "But you guys just blew it!"

Chapter 12

Monday

Dear Diary,

Mary-Kate was really mad at us yesterday for almost blowing her big chance with Jake.

Luckily, she ran after him and convinced him to come back.

"Okay, can someone please explain what is going on here?" Jake asked. "Why do you kids keep following me?"

"We were just trying to investigate the veggie-burger scam," Phoebe explained.

"Huh?" Jake looked totally confused.

I was confused, too. Even more than before. Veggie-burger scam?

"We know all about it, Mr. Nakamoto," Phoebe said. "How the hotel has been putting meat in the veggie burgers . . . because you told them to do it!"

To my surprise, instead of yelling at Phoebe, Jake burst out laughing. "That is so funny," Jake said. "A veggie-burger scam!"

Mary-Kate glared at me, then at Phoebe.

"Are you saying that you don't know anything about it?" Phoebe asked, putting her hands on her hips.

"Uh, no," Jake replied.

"Wait a minute. What *were* you doing in the rose garden restaurant's kitchen yesterday?" I asked.

"If you girls must know," Jake said, "I'm opening a sports restaurant here at the resort. I was going over the menu with the chef. He's going to start at my place as soon as it opens."

"So you *are* going to put meat in the veggie burgers," I said slowly. "But that's lying. It's false advertising."

"Not to mention totally gross," Phoebe put in.

"It's a brand-new recipe for a Nakamoto burger,"

Jake told us, throwing up his hands. "It's a veggie *hamburger*! It has meat *and* vegetables in it, which means less fat but great taste!"

Phoebe just stood there with her mouth hanging open. I felt really sorry for her. Her big story wasn't really a story at all. She probably felt totally stupid!

"A veggie hamburger. That an awesome idea!" Mary-Kate said eagerly. "When does your restaurant open? Can we go?"

"It's opening next month," Jake went on. "In fact, we had a huge outdoor photo shoot here last week for the upcoming publicity campaign. We were trying to keep it top secret. But the crew used so many bright, flashing lights that a bunch of hotel guests turned up to see what was going on."

I gulped. "Bright lights?" I said. "That shoot wasn't in the rose garden, was it?"

Jake nodded. "Yup."

That meant Elise and Summer's "UFO" was really flashbulbs from Jake's photo shoot!

"I'd really appreciate it if you kept this information to yourselves for another week," Jake said. He wagged his finger at Phoebe and me. "Especially you two."

"I'll make sure they do," Mary-Kate chimed in.

Phoebe looked at me. "So much for my big undercover story," she said. "I was planning to sell it to *The Hawaii Journal*."

"Not *The National Inquisitor*?" I asked her.

Phoebe grinned. "That worthless waste of good paper? Not if it was the last newspaper in the galaxy!"

Dear Diary,

I can't believe Phoebe thought Jake was part of a veggie-burger scam. And Ashley thought Phoebe thought Jake was an alien!

When Phoebe told Jake her side of the story, he cracked up. And when Phoebe heard Ashley's story about her, she started rolling around the sand in hysterics. I couldn't help laughing, too.

But all's well that ends well.

Jake said that he still wanted to give me that autograph.

He wrote:

FOR MY NUMBER ONE FAN, CAMPBELL
WITH BEST WISHES,
JAKE NAKAMOTO

And then he wrote another one for *me*!

"Thanks, Jake!" I said as he handed it to me. Then I had a great idea. "Phoebe, can I borrow your video camera?" I asked.

"Sure," Phoebe said, handing it over.

I turned to Jake. "I know you've already done me a huge favour," I said. "But would you mind saying hello to Campbell on tape for me?"

Jake didn't even hesitate. "Sure, why not?"

I clicked on the camera. Jake posed in front of the rolling waves and the sunrise and began talking into the camera.

"Hey, Campbell! This is Jake Nakamoto. I heard

you're really into baseball. It's good to know there are fans like you out there, cheering me on. It helps me to play my best!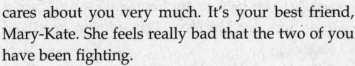

"I'm talking to you now because of someone who cares about you very much. It's your best friend, Mary-Kate. She feels really bad that the two of you have been fighting.

"It would mean a lot to me if you could give her a break. Because it would be a shame if the two of you weren't friends anymore.

"Anyway, keep hitting those home runs, Campbell! And thanks for being such a big fan!"

I clicked the camera off. "That was awesome!" I cried. I couldn't help it. I gave Jake a huge hug.

Jake smiled. "I hope everything works out."

"I know it will," I told him. And I meant it.

If this didn't win Campbell back, nothing would!

Chapter 13

Tuesday

Dear Diary,

This is our last night on Kauai. Tomorrow we're heading back to New Hampshire. From there we're all taking separate flights back to our hometowns. And then it will be Summer Vacation: Part Two in good old Chicago!

After I finished packing, I went to visit Phoebe in her room.

I knocked on her door.

"Come in!" Phoebe called.

I went inside. Phoebe was sitting at her desk,

 leafing through her notebook. Her suitcase and duffel bag were on the floor, all closed up. I noticed that her trendy outfits were sticking out of the waste-basket.

"You're not going to throw those out, are you?" I said in horror.

Phoebe shrugged. "You can have them if you want. They were just my disguises. I was trying to blend in with all the other hotel guests."

I rescued the clothes and tucked them under my

arm. "So what are you doing now? I'm really sorry you didn't get your big story."

Phoebe grinned. "Are you kidding me? I did!"

"What do you mean?" I asked.

"You don't think the story behind Jake Nakamoto's new restaurant is a good idea?" Phoebe asked. "For when it opens, I mean?"

"Hey, yeah," I said. "Sounds great!"

"And guess what he's going to call the restaurant?" Phoebe asked. "Planet Jake!"

The door burst open, and Summer and Elise rushed in. Summer was carrying two new metal hats. Elise was carrying a big makeup mirror.

Before Phoebe and I could react, Summer slipped the hats on both of us. Elise held up the mirror, then started chanting:

"Mirabilis yokum sageonis filatis. Mirabilis yokum sageonis filatis . . ."

Phoebe yanked off her hat and stood up. "You guys don't understand. Ashley and I are *fine*!"

"That's what the aliens want you to think," Elise told us.

I rolled my eyes. Even when they heard the truth,

I had a feeling Summer and Elise were still going to believe in aliens!

Dear Diary,

After dinner I went back to my room to grab Jake's autograph and video for Campbell. I was really nervous about giving them to her. What would she say?

Before I had a chance to do that, though, there was a knock at my door.

You'll never believe who it was, Diary. Campbell!

"Campbell?" I said, totally surprised. "What are you doing here?

"Please let me in, just for a second," she pleaded. "I have something I need to tell you."

I opened the door wider.

Campbell hesitated, then stepped into the room.

I took a deep breath and waited to hear what she had to say.

"I've been a real jerk, Mary-Kate," she burst out. "I was hurt, but I had no right to act that way. Can you ever forgive me?"

I stood there for a minute in total shock. Campbell was apologising to me? I didn't know what to say.

"Well, I don't blame you for hating me,"

Campbell said. She headed for the door. "I'll just leave."

"No, wait," I said. "Campbell, of course I forgive you. But do you forgive me?"

"Are you kidding?" Campbell said. "I've missed you so much! I wanted to apologise sooner, but after the way I acted, I didn't think you'd ever talk to me again."

"Really?" I asked. "I missed you, too."

We gave each other a huge hug.

Then I took the autograph off my dresser and handed it to Campbell. "Here," I said. "I got this for you."

Campbell gasped when she saw what it was. "How?" she exclaimed. "Jake's bodyguards said he wasn't signing autographs!"

"Let's just say I tried really, really hard," I said with a grin.

Campbell broke into a smile. "Wow, thanks, Mary-Kate! That's so nice of you."

I decided it was time for Present Number Two. I reached into my backpack again and pulled out the videotape.

"I have something else for you," I said. I popped

the tape into the VCR, turned on the TV, and hit Play. Jake's face filled up the screen.

Campbell ran up to the screen to get a closer look.

When the tape was finished, I hit the stop button. Campbell looked a little stunned. Then she swiped at her eyes. "Th-th-this is amazing," she sputtered. "Only a really good friend – the best friend in the whole world – would do something like this!"

She reached over and hugged me again. I hugged her back.

"I'm so glad we're friends again!" Campbell cried.

"Me, too," I agreed. We slapped palms. I had my best bud back!

We ordered chocolate-fudge ice cream from room service – Campbell's treat – and watched Jake's video about forty-nine more times.

"It's too bad we have to say goodbye for the summer just when we made up," I said.

Campbell grinned. "Don't worry! We'll have a blast when we're roommates again in September."

"Count on it!" I told her.

I never thought I would say this, Diary, but I can't wait for school to start again!

mary-kateandashley

TWO of a kind ™

Closer Than Ever

by Judy Katschke

from the series created by Robert Griffard
& Howard Adler

HarperCollins*Entertainment*
An Imprint of HarperCollins*Publishers*

A PARACHUTE PRESS BOOK

CHAPTER ONE

"Is that a new sweater, Ashley?" Mary-Kate Burke asked her sister during lunch on Friday. "It's so cool!"

"Thanks," Ashley said, glancing at her coral top. "But it isn't new. I got it over a month ago."

Mary-Kate stared at the sweater. *Weird*, she thought. *I don't remember ever seeing it before.* "Oh, well," she said with a shrug. "It's still awesome."

Mary-Kate smiled as she took a bite of her tuna sandwich. Lunch always seemed to taste better when she ate with Ashley. And it was the first time she and Ashley had got to eat together in weeks. That's because their first year at the White Oak Academy for Girls was jam-packed. There were classes, tons of homework, clubs, and sports. And sometimes they even had dates with the guys from Harrington, the all-boys school down the road!

"How are your soccer games coming along, Mary-Kate?" Ashley asked, lifting her turkey sandwich to her mouth.

"Soccer?" Mary-Kate asked. "Soccer ended last week."

"Are you serious?" Ashley cried. "Why didn't you tell me? I didn't get a chance to see any of your games and—"

"Okay, time out," Campbell Smith cut in. "What's up with you guys?"

Mary-Kate turned to her roommate. Campbell was sitting next to Phoebe Cahill across the table from her and Ashley. "What do you mean?" she asked.

"I mean, where have you two been?" Campbell asked. She brushed aside the bangs of her short brown hair. "I thought you two knew everything about each other."

"I do," Mary-Kate said. "I know Ashley is twelve and in the First Form like me. She has blonde hair, blue eyes—"

"Too easy," Phoebe piped in. Phoebe knew everything about Ashley, too. She was her roommate.

"Okay." Mary-Kate began counting on her fingers. "I know that Ashley likes purple nail polish, ballet, mayonnaise on her turkey sandwiches—"

"I switched to mustard," Ashley interrupted. "And I just ditched my purple polish."

Whoa, Mary-Kate thought. Maybe she didn't know everything there was to know about Ashley. And she was pretty sure she knew why.

"It's been so long since Ashley and I hung out together," Mary-Kate complained. "No wonder we're clueless about each other."

"Mary-Kate is right," Ashley agreed. "I've been so busy, the only person I see on a regular basis is my roommate."

"And what's wrong with that?" Phoebe asked, pretending to look hurt.

"Nothing," Ashley admitted. She turned to Mary-Kate. "It's just that I thought I'd see more of you in boarding school, Mary-Kate, not less. So I'm really starting to miss you."

Mary-Kate felt the same way. Not seeing Ashley was the pits! "I miss you, too, Ashley," she said.

"Okay, okay," Campbell said. "Now that we're all warm and fuzzy, let's get with the programme. There's got to be a way for the two of you to spend more time together."

"How?" Mary-Kate asked. "I'm on the softball team and in the drama club. . . "

"I'm on the school paper," Ashley said, "and in the cooking club. . . "

"And don't forget the Ross Lambert fan club," Phoebe said with a smile.

Ashley blushed. Ross was her boyfriend!

"How can Ashley and I do all those things," Mary-Kate said, "and still hang out together?"

The girls were silent as they thought.

Suddenly Mary-Kate had a major idea. "Hey!" she cried. "What if Ashley and I became roomies? For a whole week!"

"Share a room?" Ashley gasped. "You mean like we did back home in Chicago?"

Mary-Kate nodded. "Remember the time we pitched that tent in the middle of our room?" she asked.

"And tried to roast marshmallows with our hair dryer?" Ashley laughed.

Mary-Kate turned to Campbell and Phoebe. "You guys wouldn't mind rooming together for a week, would you?" she asked.

Campbell and Phoebe looked at each other and shrugged.

"Sounds good to me," Campbell said.

"Me, too," Phoebe said. "But do you think Miss Viola will go for the idea?"

Miss Viola was the housemother at Porter House, the girls' dorm.

"I bet she will," Mary-Kate replied. "Then it will be all systems go!"

"Speaking of going," Ashley said. She took one last bite of her sandwich and stood up. "I've got to run to the Food Management Centre and whip up my secret-recipe apple cider for the Harvest Festival tomorrow."

Mary-Kate smiled. Every October White Oak and Harrington celebrated fall in a huge way. For seven days the campus would be jumping with hayrides, pumpkin carving, touch football on the lawn, and the annual apple cider contest.

"You'll win that contest for sure, Ashley," Mary-Kate said. "Your apple cider rules."

"Thanks to my secret recipe," Ashley said.

"Oh, yeah?" Campbell replied. "What's the secret?"

Ashley flashed a mysterious smile. "It's one super-special ingredient," she said. "But if I told you, it wouldn't be a secret recipe."

Mary-Kate watched as Ashley left the dining room. She couldn't wait to start rooming with her sister again!

"You guys, I am so psyched about this," Mary-Kate told her friends. "First thing Ashley and I are going to do is stay up for hours after lights-out – just to catch up."

Phoebe laughed. "You wish."

"What do you mean?" Mary-Kate asked.

"Ashley doesn't stay up late any more," Phoebe explained. "For the last few months she's been going to bed super-early. Sometimes even before lights-out."

"Really?" Mary-Kate asked. That was new. Was there anything else about Ashley she didn't know?

"Oh, and Ashley's wardrobe is so stuffed with her clothes," Phoebe went on, "it's about to explode!"

"You have lots of clothes, too, Phoebe," Mary-Kate pointed out.

"Vintage clothes don't take up that much room," Phoebe said. "Well, at least it doesn't seem that way."

Phoebe loved dressing in clothes from the 1950s, '60s, and '70s. Even her eyeglass frames were from an antiques boutique.

"Are you sure you want to make the switch, Mary-Kate?" Campbell asked.

"You'll have to be really quiet when Ashley's sleeping. And you'll have nowhere to put your stuff," Phoebe added. "There's still time to get out of it."

"Why would I want to get out of it?" Mary-Kate asked. "Ashley's my sister. And I bet I can get her to change back to the way she was before."

"I bet you can't!" Phoebe said. Her dark curls bobbed as she shook her head.

"Me, too!" Campbell put in.

Mary-Kate wanted to laugh out loud. Were they kidding? Sure she could get Ashley to change. No problem!

"The bet is on," Mary-Kate declared. "First I'll get Ashley to stay up past midnight. Next I'll get her to give away half of her clothes."

"In your dreams!" Campbell cried.

"But you can't tell Ashley about the bet," Phoebe declared. "Not until it's over. It wouldn't be fair. She'd change on purpose to help you."

Mary-Kate gave it a thought. Keeping a secret from Ashley would be hard – especially if they were in the same room. But Mary-Kate was up to the challenge.

"Fine," she said. "But what happens to the loser of the bet . . . or in this case, losers?"

"Let me think," Campbell said. She tapped her chin with one finger. Then she snapped her fingers.

"I know! The loser has to do the winner's laundry for a month. Stinky gym socks and all!"

Mary-Kate gulped when she thought of Campbell's gym socks. Campbell was on a ton of sports teams. Which meant that by the end of the week she had a ton of stinky socks. But what was she thinking? Of course she was going to win!

"Great!" Mary-Kate said with a smile. "But get ready for me to win!"

CHAPTER TWO

"This festival rocks!" Elise Van Hook told Ashley on Saturday morning.

Ashley smiled as she looked around the campus. Students from White Oak and Harrington were crunching through red, yellow and orange leaves as they munched on toffee apples and popcorn. Music boomed over a loudspeaker, and there were tons of snack and game booths.

There were three other apple cider booths aside from Ashley's. They belonged to Felicia Jimenez, Owen McDonald and Logan Beecham.

Ashley adjusted the sign hanging on her own cider booth. It was painted white and decorated with red paper apples and pink hearts and read:

Spice Up Your Life with Ashley's Apple Cider!

"Thanks for helping me, Elise," Ashley said as she poured cider into paper cups. "Just don't spill any glitter into the cider, okay?"

Elise was a total glitter freak. She wore glitter makeup and glitter clothes. She even used glittery toothpaste!

"I went easy on the glitter today," Elise said. She leaned on the counter of the booth and sighed. "Now if you only had some customers."

"Tell me about it," Ashley groaned. She pulled up the zipper on her hooded sweatshirt. "The festival started two hours ago and so far business stinks."

Ashley looked down the row of booths. About ten kids were already lined up for Logan Beecham's apple cider.

Logan wore a white chef's hat over his spiky blond hair and an apron over his tubby stomach. He grinned as he poured cup after cup of his golden-brown cider.

Oh, great, Ashley thought. *The winning apple cider is chosen by how many kids line up for it. How can I win when everyone is lining up at Logan's booth?*

"What's Logan's secret?" Elise asked.

"Are you kidding?" Ashley asked. "Logan is the president of the Harrington Future Chefs of

America Club. He's a totally awesome cook."

Suddenly Logan stepped out from his booth. He cupped his hands around his mouth and shouted, "Might as well give up now, Burke!"

Elise put her hands on her hips. "If Logan Beecham can have a big mouth, so can we!" She leaned over the counter and shouted, "Check out Ashley's apple cider! It'll make your taste buds tingle with delight!"

Ashley giggled. "Try my apple cider!" she yelled. "It'll make your . . . tonsils tango!"

"All right!" Elise cheered.

Ashley saw Samantha Kramer and Philip Jacoby walking over. "Look who's coming," she whispered to Elise. "Samantha has had a major crush on Philip for months. But so far they're only friends."

"Bummer," Elise whispered back.

"Hi, guys," Ashley called to Samantha and Philip.

"Hi," Samantha said. "How about some of your tastebud-tingling cider?"

"Yeah," Philip said. "The line for Logan's cider is way long."

"Logan? Forget about Logan!" Elise cried. She held out two cups. "Ashley's cider is the best!"

Ashley watched as Samantha and Philip took the cups. They gulped down the cider.

"Well?" Ashley asked when they were finished. "What do you think?"

"It's really good," Philip said. He quickly turned to Samantha. "Hey, Sam. That new movie, *Big Apple Adventure,* is opening in town. Want to see it tonight?"

"Sure!" Samantha said. She gave Ashley and Elise a little wave as they walked off. "Thanks for the cider, guys!"

"Elise, I am in total shock," Ashley said. "Philip finally asked out Samantha."

"So?" Elise asked. "They *are* friends."

"News flash," Ashley declared. "Tonight is Saturday night. And Saturday night makes it an official date!"

Elise seemed to think about it. Then her eyes lit up. "Oh!" she said. "You're right!"

"Hey, Burke!" Logan called.

Ashley groaned. She turned to see him jumping up and down in front of the row of booths.

"I see you had two customers!" Logan shouted. "How much did you have to pay them to drink your cider? Ha, ha, haaaaa!"

Ashley was so angry, her cheeks burned. What was Logan's problem? Why couldn't he just leave them alone?

"Now I really want to win," Ashley said. "Just to show up Logan."

"And you *will* win," Elise said.

"With only two customers?" Ashley cried.

"Three," Elise said, pointing. "Here comes Cheryl. And she looks thirsty!"

Ashley turned. She saw her friend Cheryl Miller waving as she approached the booth.

"Hi, Cheryl," Ashley called.

"Want to try some of the world's best cider?" Elise asked.

"Bring it on!" Cheryl declared.

Ashley lifted the jug of cider and spotted Peter Juarez heading their way. Peter was a First Former at Harrington. He was also always teasing Cheryl.

"Better gulp it down fast, Cheryl," Ashley whispered. "Peter's coming."

"We know how much you hate him," Elise added. "He's always making fun of your red high-top trainers."

Ashley glanced down at Cheryl's feet. Uh-oh. She was wearing those red trainers again.

Cheryl took a small sip of the cider. She waited quietly until Peter approached the booth.

"What's up?" Peter asked. He and Cheryl exchanged a glance.

"Not much." Ashley poured him a cup of apple cider, and he took a gulp.

Cheryl took another sip of her cider. She and Peter were still eyeing each other while they drank.

Great, Ashley thought. *That's all I need – a fight right here at my booth. That should be perfect for business.*

"Hey, this is good stuff!" Peter declared.

He turned to Cheryl. But instead of insulting her, he put an arm around her shoulders!

"Want to go on the hayride?" Peter asked.

"Sure," Cheryl replied.

Ashley watched, stunned, as Cheryl and Peter walked away.

"Did you see that?" Elise cried. "Cheryl and Peter used to fight like cats and dogs. Now they're totally tight!"

"I saw it," Ashley said, shaking her head. "But I don't believe it."

Elise turned excitedly to Ashley. "Think about it, Ashley," she said. "First Samantha and Philip . . . now Cheryl and Peter. It's almost as if your apple cider is some kind of . . . love potion!"

A love potion, Ashley thought with a laugh. Now *that* would be good for business!

CHAPTER THREE

I am so psyched! Mary-Kate thought as she dragged her duffel bag towards Ashley's room. *I can't believe Ashley and I are finally going to be roommates!*

It was Saturday night. Miss Viola had said it was okay for Mary-Kate and Ashley to share a room for a week. Phoebe had already moved her stuff into Mary-Kate and Campbell's room.

Now all I have to do is get Ashley to change her habits, Mary-Kate thought, *and I'll have clean laundry for a whole month!*

Mary-Kate knocked on the door.

"Who is it?" Ashley asked from inside the room.

"Your new roommate!" Mary-Kate answered.

The door flung wide open. Ashley yanked Mary-Kate into the room and gave her a big hug.

"Mary-Kate!" Ashley cried. She began jumping up and down. "This is going to be so cool!"

"Totally," Mary-Kate agreed. But the moment she looked over Ashley's shoulder her eyes widened. A gigantic stuffed giraffe was staring at her from across the room.

"Ashley?" Mary-Kate gulped. She pointed over Ashley's shoulder. "What is that?"

Ashley turned and smiled. "Mary-Kate," she said, "meet our third roomie – Mr. Stretch!"

"Mr. Stretch?" Mary-Kate repeated. She stared at the giraffe. His huge head almost reached the ceiling, thanks to his long, wobbly neck. His eyes and tongue bulged out, and he was also the colour of old crusty mustard. Yuck!

"I picked him up at a garage sale last week," Ashley said proudly. "Isn't he way cool?"

Mary-Kate stared at the gigantic giraffe. He took up half the room. "Isn't he way . . . big?" she asked.

"Big and lovable!" Ashley said. She ran over to Mr. Stretch and hugged him around his long neck.

Uh-oh, Mary-Kate thought. *Why didn't Phoebe warn me about this?*

"Mary-Kate, I am so excited about us rooming together," Ashley said.

Okay, Mary-Kate thought. *If I'm going to start changing Ashley's habits and winning the bet, I'd better start right now.*

"Yeah," Mary-Kate said. "Now we can talk for hours and hours after lights-out."

"Oh, I don't think so," Ashley said. "Ever since we started White Oak, I've become a morning person."

"So . . . you don't stay up late any more?" Mary-Kate asked slowly.

"Not really," Ashley said. She started to yawn. "Actually, I'm getting sleepy already."

Mary-Kate stared at her sister. Phoebe wasn't kidding about Ashley's going to bed early.

"I think working that cider booth wore me out," Ashley went on. "And get this – Elise called my cider a love potion."

"A love potion?" Mary-Kate laughed. "Why does she think that?"

"Two couples got together after drinking it," Ashley said. She headed for the door. "But if you ask me, it was just a fluke."

"Hey," Mary-Kate asked, "where are you going?"

"To get washed," Ashley said. She yawned again. "And then I'm hitting the sack. I even cancelled my date with Ross because I'm so tired."

Mary-Kate glanced at the clock. It was only nine-thirty. And it was Saturday night!

This is more serious than I thought, Mary-Kate realised. How was she supposed to get Ashley to stay up past midnight?

Mary-Kate paced the room until her toe got stuck under one of Mr. Stretch's bulky feet. She gasped as she tripped and landed flat on her face.

"Ooooh!" Mary-Kate shouted. She shook a fist at Mr. Stretch. "I do *not* like you!"

She sat up and leaned against the bed. She tried to think of a way to make Ashley stay awake past midnight.

Ashley could stay up all night studying for a big killer test, Mary-Kate thought. *Nah. Ashley would probably want a good night's sleep instead.*

Or I could pretend to snore – super-loud, Mary-Kate decided. *Nah. I already snore. And that never kept her awake.*

Then suddenly it clicked. . .

"Hey!" Mary-Kate said. "I'll have a party after lights-out. That should keep Ashley pumping past midnight!" She was interrupted by a knock on the door. "Who is it?" she called.

"It's your ex-roomie," Campbell said.

"And company," Phoebe added. "I can't believe I'm knocking on my own door."

"Come in," Mary-Kate called back.

"I see you've met Mr. Stretch," Phoebe said as she and Campbell entered the room. "Gross, isn't he?"

"How could I miss him?" Mary-Kate grumbled as she stood up. "So how do you two like being roommates?"

"It's cool," Campbell said.

Phoebe nodded. "I found out Campbell has a vintage football jersey from 1970." She modelled a blue and white shirt that had the number thirteen on the back.

"It was my dad's lucky jersey," Campbell explained. "So he never washed it."

Phoebe stared at her shirt in horror. "And you made me wear it?" she cried.

Campbell laughed. "I'm kidding!"

Mary-Kate laughed, too. She knew Campbell and Phoebe would hit it off.

"By the way, Mary-Kate," Campbell said, "we saw Ashley on her way to the showers. She looked tired."

"Really tired!" Phoebe teased. "In fact, I think I even saw her yawn."

"Big deal," Mary-Kate said, waving a hand. "I came up with a great way to prove that Ashley can stay up past midnight."

"You did?" Phoebe asked.

"Spill it," Campbell said.

Mary-Kate grinned from ear to ear. "Tomorrow night I'm going to throw a party," she explained. "A roomie reunion party."

"A party, huh?" Campbell said.

"And I'd like to throw it in your room," Mary-Kate said. "If it's okay with you guys."

"Okay with me," Phoebe said, shrugging.

"Me, too," Campbell said.

"Awesome!" Mary-Kate exclaimed. "We'll have crisps, dip, music—"

"You're missing one thing," Campbell cut in.

"What?" Mary-Kate asked.

"Ashley!" Campbell said. "You'll never get her to come."

"Especially after a whole Sunday of pouring apple cider," Phoebe agreed.

But Mary-Kate wasn't worried. Since when did Ashley turn down an excuse for a good party?

"Ashley will be there," Mary-Kate insisted. "Just you wait!"

CHAPTER FOUR

"Thanks for helping me carry the cider, Mary-Kate," Ashley said on her way to her booth. She and Mary-Kate were each swinging two plastic jugs of cider as they made their way across campus.

The festival had started a few minutes earlier. Tons of kids were already filing through the yellow and red balloon arch toward the booths and games.

"By the way, Ashley," Mary-Kate said. "There's going to be a roomie reunion tonight in Campbell and Phoebe's room. There'll be crisps and dip, music, some goofy games—"

"A party?" Ashley cried. "On a Sunday night?"

"A secret party," Mary-Kate whispered.

Ashley smiled. A roomie reunion *did* sound like a

neat idea. "Okay," she said. "I'll be there."

"Really?" Mary-Kate squeaked. "It's going to be after lights-out. It might even go past midnight. Are you sure you can stay up?"

Ashley shrugged. "Pretty sure."

"Cool!" Mary-Kate said.

Elise was already stacking paper cups when they reached Ashley's cider booth. Mary-Kate plunked her two jugs on the ledge and whispered to Ashley, "Sneak over to Campbell and Phoebe's room at ten-thirty tonight, okay?"

"I'm there," Ashley said.

"Great!" Mary-Kate cried. She waved as she ran off. "See you tonight, Ashley!"

Wow, Ashley thought. *Mary-Kate sure is psyched about this roomie reunion. I wonder if she misses Campbell.*

But Ashley didn't have time to think about the party. She had a cider booth to run!

"Hi, Elise," Ashley said, leaning over the counter. "Ready for business?"

Elise nodded. She pointed to a huge cup filled with cinnamon sticks. "And I set these up like you asked," she said. "Is cinnamon your secret ingredient, Ashley?"

"No." Ashley giggled. "But nice try! I just

thought it was a cool touch. Kids can put them in their cider if they want."

She was about to enter her booth when her boyfriend, Ross Lambert, came by. His brown hair hung over one eye, and he looked really cute in his faded jeans and denim jacket.

"Hi, Ross!" Ashley said. She was always happy to see him. "What's up?"

"Just wanted to wish you luck," Ross said, "and to try some of your prizewinning apple cider."

"I didn't win yet, Ross!" Ashley laughed. She gave him a cup and watched him gulp it down.

"So, Ross?" Elise asked. "What do you think of Ashley's apple cider?"

"It's sweet," Ross said. He leaned over and gave Ashley a kiss on the cheek. "Just like the cook. See you later, Ashley."

Ashley floated on a cloud as Ross waved and walked away.

"Yo, Burke!"

Ashley slowly turned around. Logan Beecham was standing just a few feet away. He was wearing a baker's hat and an apron that read: Beecham's Cider – good to the core!

"Now what, Logan?" Ashley asked.

Logan snapped his fingers. A boy dashed out

from inside his booth. It was Logan's roommate, Carl, holding a tray of brownies.

"Starting today, a free brownie will come with each cup of my apple cider," Logan announced.

"With nuts!" Carl added.

"I put two types of nuts into the batter," Logan said. "Pecans and walnuts . . . "

Ashley shook her head. "No fair, Logan!" she declared. "This is supposed to be a cider contest!"

Logan narrowed his eyes. "If you can have cinnamon sticks," he said, "I can have brownies."

"Don't worry, Ashley," Elise said as Logan and Carl marched back to their booth. "As soon as word gets out about your cider, we'll wipe the floor with Logan!"

"Yeah!" Ashley said. She took her place in the booth. She could see about six kids heading towards them already.

Maybe Elise is right, Ashley thought.

Soon more and more kids were flocking to her cider booth. Within two hours Ashley had about thirty thirsty customers.

"Coming right up!" Ashley called to the mob as she poured cup after cup of cider. Good thing Mary-Kate helped her lug all those jugs.

"What did I tell you?" Elise asked as she emptied the third jug. "Is this great or what?"

Ashley nodded. It sure was. But something wasn't adding up. . .

"Elise?" Ashley said. "Have you noticed something weird about our customers?"

"Weird?" Elise asked. "What do you mean?"

"Most of them ask for two cups of apple cider," Ashley said, "instead of one."

"Hmm. It must be because it's so good," Elise said. "One cup of your awesome cider isn't enough, Ashley!"

"Thanks," Ashley said. "But I still don't get it."

"Hi, Ashley," Alyssa Fugi said as she hurried over. "I'll have two cups of cider, please."

Two again, Ashley thought as she filled the order. *People must really love my cider.*

"And I hope it works!" Alyssa added. She grabbed the two cups and hurried off.

"Hope it works?" Ashley repeated. "Elise, what do you think she meant by that?"

"I don't know," Elise said, shrugging.

Next Jeremy Burke strolled over. Jeremy was Ashley's cousin. He was also a bit of a pain.

"Hit me!" Jeremy said. He pointed to the jug of cider and grinned.

"Jeremy, this is your fifth cup of cider," Ashley said. "Are you that thirsty?"

"It's not for me," Jeremy said. "It's for the babes!" He took a cup from Elise and ran off.

Ashley blinked. "The babes? What is he talking about?"

"Um . . . er . . . " Elise said. "Some guys give girls flowers. Maybe Jeremy gives them apple cider."

Ashley stared at Elise. She was beginning to think something was going on.

"Ashley!" A voice interrupted her thoughts.

Ashley turned and saw their friend Summer Sorenson running over. She was tugging a cute-looking guy by the arm.

"Come on, Hunter," Summer was telling him. "You have to try some of Ashley's cider. It's the best!"

Hunter didn't answer. He was too busy bopping to the beat of his radio headset.

"I'll pour you a cup," Elise offered.

"Two, please!" Summer said, flipping her blonde hair over her shoulder. She turned to Ashley and whispered, "Thanks, Ashley. I've wanted Hunter to like me for weeks!"

"Thanks for what?" Ashley asked, confused.

Summer leaned closer. "Thanks for your love potion," she whispered, her blue eyes sparkling.

"My what?" Ashley squeaked.

"As if you didn't know!" Summer laughed.

Summer and Hunter gulped down their cups of apple cider. Then they gazed into each other's eyes.

"Come on, Hunter," Summer said. "Let's carve some pumpkins into the shape of little hearts!"

"Cool," Hunter said, still bopping.

Ashley stared at Summer and Hunter as they walked off to the pumpkin-carving tent.

"If Summer thinks my cider is a love potion," Ashley thought out loud, "then maybe all those other kids think that my cider is a love potion, too."

Ashley quickly turned to Elise, who was looking everywhere except at Ashley.

"That's it!" Ashley cried. "Elise, did you tell everyone that my cider was a love potion?"

"No way!" Elise cried.

"Are you sure?" Ashley pressed her.

Elise dug her right foot into the dirt and dragged it around in a circle. "Weeeeell," she said slowly, "I told people that your cider *might* be a love potion. Huge difference."

Ashley groaned. No wonder tons of kids were storming her booth. They didn't want cider – they wanted love!

"How could you do that, Elise?" Ashley demanded.

"Well, who knows?" Elise asked. "Maybe your cider is a love potion, and—"

"It's not!" Ashley cut in.

"It could be," Elise insisted. "You gave some to Ross this morning. And right after he drank it, he kissed you."

"But Ross is my boyfriend," Ashley said. "That doesn't count!"

"Okay, okay." Elise sighed. "I know your cider isn't a love potion. I just thought a little rumour would be good for business, that's all."

"Oh, Elise!" Ashley groaned.

A group of Second Formers hurried over to the booth.

"Hi." Ashley forced a smile. "Would you like a cup of apple cider? That's cider – not love potion!"

"As if!" one girl said. "Jade Fellows gave a cup to Darren Nunzio, and he just asked her to go on the hayride."

"We don't know what you put in your cider, Ashley," another girl gushed, "but it sure seems to do the trick!"

"That's it!" Ashley said. "Elise, you watch the booth while I go set the record straight."

"You mean you're going to tell everyone your cider isn't a love potion?" Elise gasped.

Ashley nodded. But just as she was about to leave, she heard a familiar voice. . .

"Ohhhhh, Burrrrrrke!"

Logan!

"My cider's going to beat your cider to a pulp!" Logan yelled. "A pulp. Get it?"

"He never lets up!" Ashley muttered.

"It's too bad, Ashley." Elise sighed. "A love potion would definitely help you beat Logan's cider."

Beat Logan? Ashley glanced towards the boy's booth. He and Carl had stuck cinnamon sticks up their noses and they were snorting like two walruses!

Ashley couldn't take it anymore. She had to put Logan in his place once and for all.

"Come to think of it," Ashley said slowly, "maybe I'll just keep my big mouth shut!"

CHAPTER
FIVE

"It's party time!" Mary-Kate cheered.

"Not so loud," Phoebe whispered. "If Miss Viola finds out we're having a party after lights-out, we'll be toast!"

Mary-Kate was pulling CDs from her rack. Campbell was blowing up balloons, and Phoebe was laying out plates of crisps and dip. Everyone was wearing her coolest pyjamas and slippers.

"Lights-out was ten minutes ago," Campbell said. "And I don't see Ashley anywhere."

"She's probably snug in her bed," Phoebe sighed. "Dreaming of blue ribbons and apple cider."

That better not be true, Mary-Kate thought. But she forced a smile. "That's what you think." She grabbed a crisp. "Ashley will be here. Trust me."

Her eyes lit up when she heard someone knock on the door. "What did I tell you?" Mary-Kate said as she hurried to the door. But when she opened it, she gasped. Ashley was leaning against the door frame. She had dark circles under her eyes, and her hair was kind of messy.

"Five hundred cups of apple cider." Ashley groaned. "And this was just the second day."

Mary-Kate felt bad for Ashley. Her sister looked totally wiped out. But at the same time, she couldn't let her fall asleep!

Mary-Kate grabbed Ashley's arm and pulled her into the room. "It's time to party on!"

"You guys." Ashley yawned. "I'm totally beat. I just came here to say I'm not up for a party."

Phoebe and Campbell both smiled.

"Good idea," Campbell said. "After all that work, you really need your sleep."

"Yeah," Phoebe added. "Because tomorrow after classes you'll have to pour lots and lots of cider."

Mary-Kate began to panic. She had to do something – fast. "You can't go to sleep!" she cried.

"Why not?" Ashley yawned again.

"Um . . . because," Mary-Kate said, "we were just about to play charades."

"Charades?" Ashley repeated.

Mary-Kate nodded. Ashley couldn't fall asleep if she had to think!

"I'll go first," Campbell suggested.

"Now pay attention, Ashley" Mary-Kate said as she, Ashley and Phoebe sat on the bed.

"Here goes," Campbell said. She pressed her palms together, then opened them up.

"It's a book!" Mary-Kate guessed.

Campbell nodded. She held up two fingers. Two words. Then she pressed her palms together again, this time against her cheek.

"Sleep?" Ashley asked wearily.

Campbell shook her head. She pointed at the night sky outside the window.

"Night? Good night?" Phoebe asked.

Uh-oh, Mary-Kate thought. Where was Campbell going with this?

Campbell pointed to the moon on her astrology poster.

"Is it . . . *Goodnight Moon*?" Ashley yawned.

"That's it!" Campbell snickered as Ashley lay back on the bed. *"Goodnight Moon!"*

Mary-Kate glared at Campbell. She'd picked a kids' bedtime book on purpose!

"You're next, Ashley," Mary-Kate said. She

grabbed Ashley's arm and pulled her off the bed.

"I don't want to play any more games," Ashley protested. "I told you. I'm tired."

"Fine," Mary-Kate said. She grabbed a bowl of dip and held it out. "Then try some of this jalapeño dip instead."

Ashley dug a nacho chip into the dip. But when she stuck it into her mouth—

"Whoa!" Ashley cried. She fanned her mouth. "This stuff is hot."

That should wake up Ashley, Mary-Kate thought. She glanced at the clock on the wall. Ten minutes to eleven. Twenty minutes down . . . one hour and ten minutes to go.

Ashley sat down on the rug with a cup of soda.

I know, Mary-Kate thought. *I'll pump Ashley with a ton of questions. That should keep her awake!*

"So, Ashley," Mary-Kate said. "How's the cider booth coming along? Do you think you'll win?"

"Well," Ashley said, "it's not so much about winning the prize any more. It's more about beating Logan Beecham."

"You mean that obnoxious First Former from Harrington?" Phoebe asked.

"Yup," Ashley said. She yawned again.

Sleep alert! Mary-Kate thought. She dipped her

fingers into Ashley's soda. Then she splashed Ashley's face.

"Hey!" Ashley sputtered. "What's the big idea?"

"You were falling asleep," Mary-Kate said.

"Duh!" Ashley said. "I told you I was beat. And I have to get up at the crack of dawn to make more cider."

"Hey, Ashley," Mary-Kate said, "why don't I help you with the cider?"

"You?" Ashley smiled. "No offence, Mary-Kate, but you're not exactly Betty Crocker."

"Are you saying I can't cook?" Mary-Kate asked.

"Let's just say that the last time you made brownies," Ashley said, "they were more black than brown!"

"So they were a little burned." Mary-Kate shrugged. She gasped as Ashley headed for the door. "Where are you going?"

"To bed!" Ashley declared. "You guys will just have to party without me."

Campbell and Phoebe grinned at Mary-Kate.

"Remember, Mary-Kate," Campbell whispered. "My gym socks get washed in hot water."

"And my beaded cardigans need to be hand washed," Phoebe said.

"Ashley – wait!" Mary-Kate blurted out.

Ashley stopped at the door. "What now?"

"Um," Mary-Kate said. Her eyes darted around the room until they landed on her 4-You poster.

4-You was her favourite group – and Ashley's!

"There's a special live 4-You concert on the radio tonight," Mary-Kate said quickly. "It starts at twelve-thirty."

Mary-Kate held her breath as Ashley's tired eyes opened wide. Mary-Kate had made up the whole concert idea. But she was totally desperate!

"Did you say 4-You?" Ashley asked. "Live?"

"From Los Angeles," Mary-Kate added. "That's why it's on so late over here in New Hampshire. It's three hours earlier in California."

"Wow!" Ashley exclaimed. She walked back into the room. "This is something I have to stay up for!"

"Really?" Mary-Kate squeaked. She wanted to jump for joy. Her idea worked!

"You bet," Ashley said. She grabbed a disk and slipped it into the CD player. "So let's get this party started!"

Campbell and Phoebe stared at Mary-Kate. From the looks on their faces she could tell they didn't buy the concert idea.

Mary-Kate grinned and gave her friends a shrug. One challenge down . . . and only one to go!

CHAPTER SIX

"Hi," Ashley said as she trudged into her English class. She plopped down at the desk in front of her friend Wendy Linden. "What's up?"

Wendy stared at her. "I know you hate Mondays, Ashley, but you look awful!"

"Thanks." Ashley sighed. "I was up at five o'clock in the morning, making apple cider. And last night I was up past midnight, waiting for a 4-You concert on the radio."

"4-You?" Wendy asked excitedly. "Was it any good?"

"Who knows?" Ashley said. "It wasn't on. Mary-Kate said she must have got the concert date wrong."

Just then Lily Vanderhoff, another classmate, stopped at Ashley's desk.

"You're going to be at your cider booth this afternoon, right, Ashley?" Lily asked.

"Sure," Ashley said. "As soon as classes are over."

"Great!" Lily said. "Because I have a huge crush on this guy in my history class. He wants to save the whales, just like I do!"

Ashley rolled her eyes as Lily walked away. Did everyone at White Oak think her cider was a love potion?

"What was that all about?" Wendy asked. "I thought you were giving out apple cider."

"You mean you haven't heard?" Ashley said. "Half the kids in school think my apple cider is a love potion."

"How come?" Wendy asked.

"Oh, because some guys asked some girls out after drinking my cider," Ashley said. She shook her head. "As if my cider had anything to do with it!"

"I wish it did," Wendy muttered.

Ashley turned around in her seat. "Why, Wendy?" she asked. "Is there someone *you* like?"

Wendy glanced around, then leaned close to Ashley. "There's this guy in my maths class," she whispered. "His name is Tyler Kelliher."

"I know Tyler," Ashley whispered back. "Doesn't he wear those crazy T-shirts? And he plays the clarinet in the Harrington School band, right?"

Wendy nodded. "I used to play the clarinet, too," she said. "I brought it up to White Oak, but I haven't opened the case in about two years."

"Cool," Ashley said. "So the two of you have something in common already."

"Big deal." Wendy sighed. "Tyler hardly knows I'm alive. I might as well be invisible."

Ashley smiled. Wendy could never be invisible. She was too much fun!

"Can you help me get Tyler's attention, Ashley?" Wendy asked.

"I'd love to help," Ashley said, "but I'm up to my neck in apple cider. I'm just too busy this week."

"I thought Elise was helping you," Wendy said.

"Elise works with me at the booth," Ashley explained. "But I could really use some help making the cider."

"Oh," Elise said. But then her eyes lit up. "I'll do it! I'm great in the kitchen. And I don't mind getting up early, either."

"Really?" Ashley asked. "That would be great."

"Come on, Ashley," Wendy said. "If you start

working on Tyler this afternoon, then I'll start working on your cider."

It was an offer Ashley couldn't refuse. "You got it," she agreed. "I'll show you my secret recipe during midday break."

"But don't let Tyler know I like him," Wendy said. "Not until we're sure he likes me."

"It's a deal!" Ashley said.

"Do you believe this incredible line?" Elise asked Ashley at the festival. "It snakes all the way back to the caramel popcorn stand!"

"I know!" Ashley said excitedly. "It's a good thing Wendy is helping us with the cider."

"You mean the love potion," Elise giggled.

"Very funny," Ashley said. While they finished setting up, she told Elise all about Wendy and Tyler.

"Yo, Burke!" a booming voice cut in.

Ashley turned to see Logan sitting inside his booth.

"I heard you put spider legs in your apple cider!" Logan shouted.

"You're so gross, Logan!" Ashley said. "You know that's not true. You're just jealous that I've got all these customers!"

"Shh!" Elise whispered. She nudged Ashley with

her elbow. "Here comes Mrs. Pritchard." Mrs. Pritchard was the headmistress at White Oak.

"Well!" Mrs. Pritchard said. She nodded at the long line. "You must have delicious apple cider, Ashley!"

"Would you like a cup, Mrs. Pritchard?" Ashley asked. She held up a jug. "It's the best!"

Mrs. Pritchard shook her head. "I'll leave the contest to the students," she said. "Keep up the good work."

"Even Mrs. Pritchard noticed," Ashley whispered excitedly to Elise. She turned back to her customers. "Next!"

"Hi," a boy said.

Ashley stared at the boy standing in front of her. He had curly black hair and was wearing a Mr. Bubble T-shirt.

"Tyler Kelliher!" Ashley gasped.

"That's me," Tyler said, smiling.

Am I lucky or what? Ashley thought. *I'll just pour Tyler some apple cider, then start talking about Wendy.*

"Have some cider, Tyler," Ashley said. She shoved a cup into his hand. "And stick around. I want to know what you think of it."

And what you think of Wendy! she silently added.

"Sure," Tyler said as he took a sip.

"So," Ashley said, "how is it?"

"This stuff is great," Tyler said.

"Have some more!" Ashley said, holding out another cup. "You know, you'll never guess who helped me with my cider, Tyler."

Tyler didn't respond.

"Um," Ashley went on. "Do you want to guess? She's a First Former like me. She's got really nice brown eyes and a great smile."

"I was wondering if maybe we could go on a date sometime, Ashley," Tyler blurted out.

Huh? Ashley jumped and splashed cider all over herself.

"Here you go," Tyler said, holding out a napkin.

But Ashley didn't care about the cider on her shirt. "What did you say?" she asked.

"I said maybe we could go out sometime," Tyler repeated.

Ashley sighed. "That's what I thought you said."

"Think about it," Tyler said. He crunched the cup in his hand and tossed it into the trash can. "See you!"

Ashley gaped at Tyler as he walked away. Something had gone terribly wrong.

"I heard that," Elise said over Ashley's shoulder. "He just asked you out!"

"But he's not supposed to ask me out," Ashley

groaned. "He's supposed to ask Wendy."

"Well, what do you expect?" Elise asked with a grin. "You're dealing with a highly effective love potion."

Ashley turned to face Elise. "Elise, quit saying that," she said. "My apple cider is not a love potion."

"Tell that to Tyler!" Elise laughed.

"Boy, do I have a problem," Ashley said. "How am I going to get Tyler to like Wendy when he seems to like me?"

CHAPTER SEVEN

"Are you sure it's that bad?" Mary-Kate asked.

"Worse than you can ever imagine," Phoebe replied. "I have to share a wardrobe with Ashley, remember?"

Mary-Kate grabbed the handle on the wardrobe door. She took a deep breath and turned to her friends. "Are you ready?" she asked. She hadn't dared to look inside Ashley's wardrobe for months, but now she had no choice.

Phoebe and Campbell both nodded.

"Then stand back!" Mary-Kate shouted as she yanked the wardrobe door open.

Everyone shrieked as shoes, sweaters, trousers, and T-shirts tumbled out.

"It's an avalanche!" Campbell cried.

When the clothes settled on the floor, Mary-Kate stared at the towering heap. "Wow. I had no idea what I was dealing with," she said.

Mary-Kate plucked one of Ashley's hats from the floor and tossed it over Mr. Stretch's horns. "Here," she told the giraffe. "Make yourself useful for a change."

Phoebe folded her arms across her chest. "So, Mary-Kate," she said. "Do you know how you're going to get Ashley to clear out half her clothes?"

Mary-Kate nodded. "I've already come up with a plan."

"What is it?" Campbell said.

"Well," Mary-Kate said. "I know for a fact that the theater department needs new clothes for the costume room."

"So?" Campbell asked.

"So I'll ask Ashley to donate some of her clothes," Mary-Kate explained.

Campbell and Phoebe stared at Mary-Kate. Then they began to laugh.

"Ashley will never part with her wardrobe," Phoebe insisted.

"Wrong!" Mary-Kate declared. "I know for a fact that Ashley loves helping a good cause. She once made fifteen cherry pies for a charity bake sale."

Mary-Kate, Campbell and Phoebe began stuffing the clothes back into the closet. When they were done, Mary-Kate glared at Mr. Stretch.

"Do you see that?" Mary-Kate asked. "He stares at me while I do my homework, while I sleep. . . What does he want from me now?"

"He's just a stuffed animal!" Campbell said.

"And you'd better deal with it, Mary-Kate," Phoebe said. "I don't like Mr. Stretch either, but Ashley loves him."

The door swung open. Ashley stepped into the room with a big yellow stain on her top.

"What happened to you?" Mary-Kate asked.

"Cider accident," Ashley sighed. She hurried towards the wardrobe. "I just need a clean shirt."

Ashley opened the wardrobe door a crack. She carefully slipped an arm inside and pulled out a salmon-coloured long-sleeved T-shirt.

Wow, Mary-Kate thought. *She's got it down to a science!*

Ashley pointed to Mr. Stretch. "Hey! Why is my hat hanging on Mr. Stretch's horns?" she asked.

Mary-Kate froze. Ashley couldn't know they were studying her wardrobe. "Um, no idea," she replied.

Ashley shrugged and stuffed the hat back into

her wardrobe. "You know," she said, "after this Harvest Festival is over, I have to go shopping for winter clothes."

"Good idea," Campbell said. "As they say, one can never have too many clothes."

Mary-Kate glared at Campbell.

"Um, Ashley," Mary-Kate said. "Where are you going to put all those new clothes once you get them?"

"Where else?" Ashley asked. "In the wardrobe."

"But you and Phoebe hardly have any room as it is," Mary-Kate pointed out. "So why don't you make room by getting rid of some of your clothes?"

While Ashley slipped into her clean shirt, Mary-Kate explained about the theatre department and the donations.

"So what do you think?" Mary-Kate asked. She held her breath while Ashley thought it over.

"I think it's a neat idea," Ashley said. "Not only will I be clearing out my part of the wardrobe, I'll be making a contribution to the White Oak theatre department!"

"That's the idea!" Mary-Kate cheered.

"But I'll have to donate the clothes late this afternoon," Ashley said. "I still have a ton of cider to give out."

Ashley left the room.

Mary-Kate turned to Phoebe and Campbell and smiled. "I win! I win!"

"Not so fast," Phoebe said. "Ashley can still change her mind."

"In fact," Campbell added slowly, "if a bunch of Ashley's clothes aren't out of this wardrobe by the end of the day, you lose."

"No problem," Mary-Kate said.

But by late afternoon, the wardrobe was still jammed.

This doesn't look good, Mary-Kate thought. *I'd better go to Ashley's booth and see what's up.*

Mary-Kate ran across campus to the Harvest Festival. When she reached Ashley's booth, she had to squeeze through a thick crowd of kids to get to the front of the line.

"Sorry, Mary-Kate," Ashley said as she poured cup after cup of cider. "I'm too busy to sort through my clothes right now. I'll have to do it tomorrow."

Tomorrow? Mary-Kate's stomach flipped.

"I have an idea!" Mary-Kate blurted out. "Let me take your clothes over to the theatre department."

"But I didn't pick them out yet," Ashley asked.

"Just tell me the ones you want to donate," Mary-Kate said, "and I'll get to work."

Ashley handed out four more cider cups.

244

"Okay," she said. "Take the old things from the back of the wardrobe. Most of the stuff is on wire hangers."

"Back of wardrobe . . . wire hangers," Mary-Kate repeated. "Got it."

Mary-Kate raced back to their room. She opened the wardrobe door. Which side was Ashley's? Mary-Kate wasn't positive, but she had a feeling it was the right side. She reached way into the back. Sure enough, there was a bunch of things on wire hangers.

She yanked out an armload of clothes, pulled them off the wire hangers, and stuffed them into a big plastic garbage bag.

This was a piece of cake! Mary-Kate thought as she dragged the bag to the theatre building.

"What's that?" Mrs. Tuttle asked as Mary-Kate dropped the bag on the costume room floor. Mrs. Tuttle was the head seamstress of the theatre department.

"Here are some clothes for future performances," Mary-Kate announced. "I'd like to donate them to the theatre department."

"Thank you, Mary-Kate," Mrs. Tuttle said. She pulled a pin out of a tomato-shaped pincushion. "We can always use more costumes for the plays."

Mary-Kate breathed a sigh of relief. Mission accomplished.

I did it! Mary-Kate thought as she walked back to Porter House. *I won the bet!*

As Mary-Kate neared her room, she spotted Phoebe waiting outside the door.

"There you are," Phoebe said. "I had to go inside my old room. But then I remembered that we switched keys."

Mary-Kate couldn't wait to tell Phoebe the news. "If you were planning to see if Ashley's clothes are still in the wardrobe," she said, "you're out of luck."

"Why?" Phoebe asked.

Mary-Kate turned her key in the lock and opened the door. "Come in and see for yourself," she said.

"Okay," Phoebe said. "But I have to get my 1970s crocheted sweater from the wardrobe."

Phoebe walked into the room and stuck her head into the wardrobe. But instead of declaring how roomy it was, she began rummaging around.

"That's funny," Phoebe said. "I could have sworn my sweater was in here."

Mary-Kate stared at Phoebe. She was going through the right side of the wardrobe – the side where Mary-Kate had taken the clothes!

"Um, Phoebe," Mary-Kate said, her voice cracking. "Do you by any chance use . . . wire hangers?"

"Sometimes," Phoebe said. "Why? Did you see my sweater?"

Mary-Kate's knees felt weak. She had donated Phoebe's clothes instead of Ashley's!

"Why don't I look for the sweater?" Mary-Kate squeaked.

"You?" Phoebe asked. "Why?"

"Because . . . er . . . I think I heard Miss Viola call your name out in the hall," Mary-Kate said quickly.

"Really?" Phoebe asked. "I must have a phone call."

"Right," Mary-Kate said. She hustled Phoebe into the hall. Then she slammed the door.

"Now I have to drag Ashley's clothes all the way to the theatre building and switch them with Phoebe's!" Mary-Kate cried.

She looked at her watch and gasped. "And the building closes in five minutes!"

CHAPTER EIGHT

Mary-Kate pulled out another plastic garbage bag. She tore through the left side of the wardrobe and stuffed the bag with some of Ashley's old clothes.

"Please let the building be open, please be open, please be open," she muttered as she dragged the bulky bag all the way across campus. But when she reached the door of the theatre building . . .

"Oh, no!" Mary-Kate cried. "It's locked!" She dropped the bag. She leaned against the door and sank to the ground. "I lost the bet!" she wailed. "I'm going to be washing stinky socks for a whole month!"

The door suddenly swung open.

"Whoa!" Mary-Kate cried as she fell into the room.

248

Mrs. Tuttle peered down at Mary-Kate. "What can I do for you now?" she asked.

Mary-Kate sprung to her feet. She still had a chance to switch the bags!

"That bag of clothes I donated before was the wrong bag, Mrs. Tuttle," Mary-Kate said quickly. She pointed to the plastic bag outside the door. "That's the right bag."

Mrs. Tuttle looked at the bag. Then at Mary-Kate. "So what do you want me to do?" she asked.

"Um," Mary-Kate squeaked. "Can I . . . switch them?"

Mrs. Tuttle shrugged. "Go ahead," she said.

"Yes!" Mary-Kate cheered. "I mean, yes, Mrs. Tuttle, that's all I need to do."

Mrs. Tuttle held the door while Mary-Kate made the switch.

"I won!" Mary-Kate sighed as she dragged Phoebe's clothes back to Porter House. "But that was close!"

"How am I going to do it?" Ashley asked Mary-Kate that night. "How am I going to get Tyler to like Wendy instead of me?"

It was fifteen minutes after lights-out. Ashley and Mary-Kate were sitting up in bed and talking.

"Maybe Tyler and Wendy can go on a hayride,"

Mary-Kate said. "Hayrides can be pretty romantic."

Ashley gave it a thought. She and Ross once went on a hayride. And it was romantic. But . . .

"Wendy is allergic to hay," Ashley sighed.

"Oh," Mary-Kate said. "Then why doesn't Wendy buy Tyler one of those gooey toffee apples?"

"I don't think so," Ashley said. "Tyler wears braces."

Mary-Kate laughed. "Bad idea!"

Ashley giggled along with her sister. They were having fun together in the same room – just like old times. So much fun that Ashley wasn't even sleepy!

"Okay, back to square one," Mary-Kate said. "Is there anything that Tyler and Wendy have in common?"

"Yeah!" Ashley exclaimed. "Wendy and Tyler both play the clarinet."

"There you go!" Mary-Kate cheered. "Now all you have to do is figure out a way to let Tyler know."

Ashley was psyched. Why hadn't she thought of the clarinet before? She was about to plan a scheme when she heard music. A soft, jazzy kind of music.

Ashley swung her legs over the side of the bed as she listened. "That's really weird," she said. "The music sounds like it's coming from outside."

"Who's playing music outside this late?" Mary-Kate asked. She jumped out of bed. But as she hurried to the window, she stumbled over one of Mr. Stretch's big stuffed feet!

"Ow!" Mary-Kate cried. "I hate that giraffe, Ashley!"

"Please. Nobody could hate Mr. Stretch!" Ashley replied. She walked to the window, lifted the blinds, and looked down.

"It's Tyler," Ashley said. He was wearing a tuxedo-print T-shirt under his black leather jacket. "And he's playing his clarinet."

Mary-Kate stared at him and giggled. "He looks like he's doing it for someone in our dorm," she said. "Just like in those old romantic movies."

Ashley gazed down at Tyler. Just then Tyler lowered his clarinet. He opened his mouth and began to sing.

"Ashley Burke . . . I must be a jerk . . . I never thought our love would work. . ."

Ashley gasped. She knew Tyler had a little crush on her – but this was crazy!

"Uh-oh," Mary-Kate said. "How are you going to get Tyler to like Wendy now?"

"Wendy?" Ashley flopped down on her bed. She threw her pillow over her head and moaned.

"Wendy lives right upstairs. She probably heard everything!"

Maybe Wendy slept through the whole thing, Ashley thought hopefully as she entered the Food Management Centre.

"Good morning, Ashley," a voice said.

Ashley spun around. Standing behind her was Wendy.

"Hi, Wendy," Ashley said as they walked into the kitchen together. "Ready to make another batch of apple cider?"

"Sure," Wendy said. "As soon as you tell me why Tyler was singing a love song to you last night."

Ashley froze. *Uh-oh,* she thought.

Ashley smiled as she tied an apron over her red sweater and black jeans. "It was probably a rhyming assignment for his songwriting class. Burke . . . jerk . . . work. It's harder to rhyme Linden."

"Nice try, Ashley," Wendy said. "But I heard the whole thing from my window. You're supposed to get Tyler to notice me – not you!"

"Look, Wendy." Ashley sighed. "The whole thing was a misunderstanding."

Wendy frowned. "I thought you were supposed to be helping me, Ashley!"

"I am!" Ashley insisted. "And I came up with the perfect plan that's sure to get you and Tyler together."

"You did?" Wendy asked. She tilted her head. "What kind of a plan?"

Ashley grinned. "Meet me at the music building this afternoon at three o'clock sharp," she said. "And don't forget your clarinet!"

CHAPTER NINE

"Excuse me!" Mary-Kate said as she dragged her overstuffed laundry bag into Campbell and Phoebe's room. "Is this the drop-off laundry service?"

It was Tuesday during midday break. Phoebe was lying on her bed, reading a magazine. Campbell was typing on her computer.

"What is all that?" Campbell asked.

"What does it look like?" Mary-Kate replied. "It's this week's laundry. I won the bet, remember?"

"How can we forget?" Phoebe said. "You've been reminding us ever since you got Ashley to donate her clothes to the theatre department."

"Didn't we hear enough bragging yesterday?" Campbell complained.

"Maybe," Mary-Kate said. "Now can I finally tell Ashley about the bet? She'll get such a kick out of it."

"To find out she was part of the bet?" Phoebe asked. She leaned back in her chair. "I don't think so!"

Mary-Kate pointed to her laundry bag. "Just remember," she said. "Make sure you wash all my red stuff separately."

"Okay, okay." Campbell groaned.

Mary-Kate smiled as she sat down on her old bed. The lumps were still in the same places. And the mattress still crunched. Just like old times!

"I can't believe it's already Tuesday," Mary-Kate sighed. "I'll be back here in my own room in no time."

"What about Ashley?" Phoebe asked. "Won't you miss rooming with her?"

"Sure," Mary-Kate said. "But there is one person I won't miss."

"Who?" Campbell asked.

"Mr. Stretch," Mary-Kate said.

"He's not a person!" Campbell laughed. "He's just a goofy stuffed giraffe."

"Don't tell that to Ashley," Mary-Kate said. "According to her, he rules the room."

"That's for sure," Phoebe replied. "Too bad we didn't make Mr. Stretch a part of the bet."

Suddenly a gleam appeared in Phoebe's eye. A smile began to spread across her face. "Why don't we reopen the bet?"

"No way," Mary-Kate declared. The mattress springs squeaked as she leaped off the bed. "The bet is over. And I won fair and square."

"I know, I know," Phoebe said. "But this time the prize will be double. If you win, then we do your laundry for *two* whole months."

Mary-Kate wasn't sure she liked the idea. What if she lost? Did that mean she had to do Campbell's and Phoebe's laundry for two months? But she wanted to hear Phoebe out.

"What do I have to do?" Mary-Kate asked.

"You have to get Ashley to give up Mr. Stretch," Phoebe said. "By Thursday after school."

"I don't know, Phoebe," Mary-Kate said.

"What's the matter?" Campbell said. "Don't think you can get rid of one little stuffed giraffe?"

"Whatever. It was just a suggestion," Phoebe said. Then she smiled. "But you know, Mary-Kate, Ashley loves that thing so much, she'll probably bring it home for winter break. And for the whole summer, too."

Mary-Kate's eyes flew wide open. Mr. Stretch? At home?

"Yeah," Campbell added. "Don't you guys share a room back in Chicago?"

"Okay, I'll do it!" Mary-Kate announced. It wouldn't be so hard. She had got Ashley to do everything so far, right?

Phoebe started to laugh.

"Hey," Mary-Kate said. "What's so funny?"

"No way will Ashley give up that giraffe," Phoebe said. "She adores him!"

"You'd better take your wash back, Mary-Kate," Campbell chuckled. "I don't think we'll be needing it anymore!"

Mary-Kate gulped as she watched her friends laughing. Of course Ashley adored Mr. Stretch. What was she thinking? How was she ever going to get Ashley to give up that giraffe?

CHAPTER TEN

"Now, remember, Wendy," Ashley said. "The plan is to show Tyler how much the two of you have in common. And that means playing the clarinet."

"But I haven't played this thing in years," Wendy said. She blew some dust off her clarinet case. "What if Tyler thinks I stink?"

"He won't," Ashley replied. "He'll be too busy wondering why he hasn't asked you out before."

Wendy raised an eyebrow. "Are you sure this is going to work?" she asked.

It better work, Ashley thought. But she flashed a confident smile. "Of course it will work!" she declared. "Trust me!"

Wendy sat on the steps of the music building.

Then she slowly opened her clarinet case.

Ashley checked her watch. It was three o'clock. "Tyler's music class ends right around now," she told Wendy. "So get ready to play."

"Thanks, Ashley," Wendy said. She smiled as she slid the reed into her clarinet. "But shouldn't you be working your cider booth?"

"Elise is watching the booth," Ashley explained. "And thanks to all the cider you helped me make, there's plenty to go around."

Wendy shut her case and held up her clarinet. "I think I'm ready," she said.

Ashley glanced over her shoulder at the music building. "I'll hide behind one of those pillars," she said. "But don't worry. I'll make sure Tyler never sees me."

Ashley slipped behind the closest pillar. She could hear Wendy begin to play a song.

Not bad, Ashley thought, peeking out. And as soon as Tyler came out, they'd be playing beautiful music together!

A few kids began to file out of the building. One of those kids was Tyler!

Ashley held her breath as he stopped behind Wendy. He shifted his clarinet case under his arm and grinned.

He's smiling! Ashley thought excitedly. *He's smiling at Wendy. The plan is working!* She strained her ears to listen.

"I didn't know you played the clarinet," Tyler said when Wendy stopped playing.

Wendy stood up and faced Tyler. "I haven't played in years," she admitted. "But I'd like to start practising again."

"Cool," Tyler said. He gave a little shrug. "Maybe we could practise together sometime."

Ashley's heart did a triple flip. He'd practically asked Wendy out on a date!

Wendy smiled. "Well—"

"Say yes!" Ashley cried.

Tyler and Wendy spun around. Ashley clapped a hand over her mouth.

"Who's there?" Tyler called.

Ashley pounded the pillar with a fist. She had blown her cover!

"H-hi," Ashley stammered as she stepped into view. "Just . . . hanging out."

"Hi, Ashley," Wendy said.

"Wow!" Tyler gushed. "I never expected to see you around the music building, Ashley!"

"Oh, I just had to see where that awesome music was coming from," Ashley said. She turned to Tyler.

"Did you hear how well Wendy plays the clarinet?"

"Sure did," Tyler said.

"I can hardly believe that she hasn't practised in years!" Ashley went on.

"Me either," Tyler said with a shrug.

"In fact," Ashley continued, "I wish I could play the clarinet just like Wendy. She's awesome!"

"Hey," Tyler said. "Maybe I could teach you how to play the clarinet, Ashley."

Ashley stared at Tyler. "What?"

"What?" Wendy cried.

Tyler nodded at Ashley. "We can meet during midday break," he said. "Or maybe even after school every day!"

Ashley began to panic. Her master plan was tanking!

"Thanks, Tyler," Ashley said quickly. "But with my cider booth and everything, I'm too busy during my breaks, and after school—"

"The Harvest Festival ends on Saturday," Tyler said. "So why don't we get together this Saturday night?"

"S-S-Saturday night?" Ashley stammered. "As in date night?"

"Yeah," Tyler said. "Unless you're already busy?"

"As a matter of fact, I am!" Ashley cried. "My boyfriend, Ross, mentioned going to the movies."

"Boyfriend?" Tyler asked. His smile turned into a frown. "Oh. Okay."

Ashley watched as Tyler trudged down the steps of the music building.

"Wait, Tyler!" Ashley called. "Aren't you and Wendy going to—"

Wendy jabbed Ashley with an elbow. "Forget it, Ashley. It's obvious who Tyler likes. And it's not me. Thanks for trying, though."

Ashley watched silently as Wendy packed up her clarinet. She felt awful. Wendy had gone out of her way to help her, but Ashley hadn't held up her end of the deal at all.

I've got to fix this, Ashley thought. *I've got to get Tyler and Wendy together if it's the last thing I do!*

CHAPTER ELEVEN

"So, Mary-Kate," Campbell said in the dining room on Tuesday night. "Have you thought of a brilliant way to get Ashley to ditch Mr. Stretch?"

"Well," Mary-Kate said, "I'm going to tell Ashley about that soft-toy drive over at the children's hospital. I told you she loves to help good causes."

Campbell tore off a piece of her onion roll. "That is a good idea, Mary-Kate," she said.

"And it's a good cause," Mary-Kate added.

"There's just one problem," Phoebe said. "All of the soft animals have to be teddy bears for the hospital's annual teddy bear picnic."

"Teddy bears?" Mary-Kate groaned.

"Face it, Mary-Kate," Campbell said. "You're not

even anywhere close to getting rid of Mr. Stretch."

"Not true," Mary-Kate argued. "I have tons of great ideas. She tapped her head with one finger. "They're all in here."

Deep inside, Mary-Kate knew her friends were right. So far she had nothing. But she was not about to give up!

Mary-Kate finished her dinner and hurried back to her room. She had only one day to get Ashley to ditch Mr. Stretch!

If I stare at Mr. Stretch for hours, Mary-Kate thought as she opened the door, *something has got to click.*

Switching on the light, Mary-Kate gasped.

Ashley was sprawled on her bed with an open bag of chocolate chip cookies at her side.

Mary-Kate knew what that meant. Ashley always broke out the chocolate chip cookies when she was having a major crisis.

"Uh-oh," Mary-Kate said. "What's wrong?" She sat on the bed next to her. "Is it the cider?"

"That's the least of my problems," Ashley sighed. "It's Tyler Kelliher," she said. "The more I try to get him to like Wendy, the more he likes me!"

"Doesn't he know you already have a boyfriend?" Mary-Kate asked.

"He does now." Ashley sighed. "But what difference does it make? Wendy has totally given up."

Mary-Kate watched as Ashley dug into the cookie bag. With Ashley so upset, how could Mary-Kate bring up Mr. Stretch?

"I'm sorry, Ashley," Mary-Kate said slowly. "If there's anything I can do for you—"

"There is!" Ashley interrupted. She sat up and pointed to Mary-Kate's side of the room. "You can start by cleaning up your mess."

"Mess?" Mary-Kate glanced at the books and clothes spread out on her bed. The sports equipment piled on her dresser. The balled-up tissues scattered on the floor. Her overflowing laundry bag. "What mess?"

"I love sharing a room with you, Mary-Kate," Ashley said. "But I forgot how messy your side can be. I mean, there's practically no room for any of my stuff!"

I'm *taking up too much room?* Mary-Kate immediately thought of Mr. Stretch.

"You know, Ashley," Mary-Kate said. "Maybe it's not my stuff that's taking up all the room."

"What do you mean?" Ashley demanded.

"Maybe if the room was less cluttered," Mary-

Kate said, "it wouldn't seem so messy."

Casually, Mary-Kate walked around the room. "For example," she said. "You can start by adding some more bookshelves above your desk."

Ashley nodded. "It's possible."

"And you can replace your bulky beanbag chair with a sleek, foldable butterfly chair," Mary-Kate went on.

"Good idea," Ashley replied.

"And . . . " Mary-Kate said slowly. "You might want to think about getting rid of the biggest thing in the room."

"What's that?" Ashley asked.

Mary-Kate shrugged. "Mr. Stretch?"

Ashley's eyes popped wide open. She ran to Mr. Stretch and wrapped her arms around his long, wobbly neck.

"No way!" Ashley said. "I would never give up Mr. Stretch!"

Mary-Kate gaped at Ashley as her sister hugged the goofy giraffe. There was no way she was going to win this bet. Why didn't she stop it while she still had the chance?

Now, for the next two months she'd be washing tons and tons of dirty, stinky laundry!

CHAPTER TWELVE

"Thanks for helping me carry the cider again, Mary-Kate," Ashley said as they both plunked crates of cider jugs inside Ashley's booth. It was Wednesday afternoon and the Harvest Festival was still going strong.

"No problem," Mary-Kate said. She pretended to flex her biceps. "I don't work out with the girls' softball team for nothing."

Ashley giggled. With all the trouble she was having with Tyler, it was great to see more of Mary-Kate!

"Well, good luck today," Mary-Kate said. She walked away.

Ashley turned and saw Elise pushing her way through the festival crowd. Elise was carrying another big cup of cinnamon sticks.

"Way to go, Ashley," Elise said as she entered the booth. She pointed to the jugs of apple cider. "That's enough cider to feed an army. We won't run out today!"

"Yeah," Ashley sighed.

Elise tilted her head as she studied Ashley for a minute. "Ashley?" she asked slowly. "Why do you look so bummed out? Didn't Wendy help you this morning?"

"That's the problem," Ashley wailed. "She did

help me make the cider. And so far I've done nothing to help her."

Elise shook her head. "Why don't you just tell Tyler that Wendy likes him – once and for all?"

"I can't," Ashley said. "I promised Wendy I wouldn't tell Tyler until we knew for sure he liked her."

"Okay," Elise said. "But this will cheer you up, Ashley. Check out the kids lining up at your booth!"

Ashley smiled when she saw the crowd. "Wow," she whispered. "I can't believe they still think my cider is a love potion."

"Who cares?" Elise whispered back. "Just keep thinking about that blue ribbon on Saturday. And about beating the pants off Logan Beecham."

Ashley nodded. But then she realised something. "Oh, Elise!" she said. "I forgot to bring extra packages of paper cups. I'll just run to the—"

"Yo, Burke!"

Ashley looked up and saw Logan shoving his way to the front of the line. What now?

"Hello, ladies!" Logan said. He leaned over the counter and grinned.

"What do you want, Beecham?" Elise demanded. "Can't you see we're busy?"

"Which is exactly why I came over," Logan said.

"I want to see what all the fuss is about."

"What do you mean?" Ashley asked.

Logan held out one hand. "A cup of Ashley's apple cider, please!" he said.

Ashley narrowed her eyes at Logan. Why did he want to try her cider? So he could figure out her secret recipe?

"Don't do it, Ashley," Elise muttered. "He doesn't deserve your cider."

"If you don't give me a cup," Logan said in a singsong voice, "I'll tell Mrs. Pritchard!"

The last thing Ashley wanted was to get in trouble with Mrs. Pritchard.

"Okay, okay," Ashley said. She poured some cider into a cup and handed it to Logan. "Knock yourself out."

Logan sniffed the cider. Then he took a sip and began swishing it inside his mouth.

"Well?" Elise asked. She placed her hands on her hips. Logan stopped swishing. Then—

"Pfleeeech!"

"Ewww!" The crowd jumped back as Logan spit a stream of apple cider to the ground.

Ashley stood frozen. She couldn't believe Logan could be so creepy!

"It needs something," Logan said as he walked

away. "Maybe another pinch of spider legs."

Ashley was steaming mad. But no way would she let Logan Beecham get the better of her.

"Forget him, Elise," Ashley muttered. "I'm going to run to the Student U for more cups."

Ashley raced to the Student Union. She was about to head to the supply closet, when she spotted Tyler. He was listening to a portable CD player as he pasted flyers on the wall.

Maybe there's still a chance, Ashley thought. *Maybe I can still get Tyler to like Wendy. It's worth one last try.*

Ashley flashed a big smile as she walked over. "Hi, Tyler!" she called. "What are you listening to?"

Tyler pulled off his earphones. "It's 'Keep It Real,' by the Wingnuts!" Tyler said. He pointed to his Wingnuts T-shirt. "I really like them. Do you?"

Ashley did. But the last thing she wanted was another reason for Tyler to like her.

"No way!" Ashley snapped. She marched over to the cabinet and began pulling out paper cups. "I hate the Wingnuts. In fact, I think they totally reek!"

Tyler began to laugh. "Don't worry, Ashley," he said. "I know you have a boyfriend."

Ashley blushed. Tyler had got the message yesterday. And he was being a good sport about it, too.

"What flyers are you hanging up, Tyler?" Ashley asked. "Something cool happening?"

"Yup!" Tyler said. He walked over and taped a flyer to the cabinet. "My music club is having a karaoke party. It's here in the Union tonight at eight."

"Karaoke?" Ashley asked. "Sounds like fun." *And like the perfect way to get Tyler and Wendy together,* she thought.

"Think you'll be there?" Tyler asked.

"I am so there!" Ashley said as she carried the paper cups to the door. "And I might even bring a friend!"

*   *   *

"Thanks for telling me about this, Ashley," Wendy said that night. "The last time I tried karaoke I had a blast."

Ashley and Wendy walked together to the Student Union. If Ashley had told Wendy about Tyler, she might not have come. So she decided to surprise her instead.

"Karaoke is cool," Ashley said. "Where else can you grab a mike and pretend you're a superstar?"

The Student U was already jumping with kids from White Oak and Harrington. Tyler was working the karaoke machine while a group of

Second Form boys sang a number by 4-You.

"Oh, no, Ashley," Wendy whispered. "Tyler's here! What do I do?"

"Just be yourself," Ashley whispered back. She saw Tyler wave from across the room. He was wearing a T-shirt decorated with musical notes.

"Ashley, Wendy!" Tyler called. He held up the mike. "Want to give it a shot?"

"Not me, thanks," Ashley said.

"Wendy?" Tyler asked. "Are you as good at singing as you are with the clarinet?"

Wendy blushed. "Well, I—"

"Wen-dy! Wen-dy! Wen-dy!" the other kids began to chant.

"Go for it," Ashley told her.

Wendy smiled, stepped forward, and took the mike from Tyler.

"So what tune will it be?" Tyler asked.

"I don't know." Wendy shrugged. "How about . . . 'Keep it Real,' by the Wingnuts?"

"The Wingnuts!" Tyler said. He pressed a few buttons on the controls. "An excellent choice!"

For sure, Ashley thought. *Those two have more in common than I thought!*

Ashley watched the TV screen as a music video appeared. Soon the lyrics were displayed on the bottom of the screen. Wendy began to sing.

"'I never wanted you to love me. . . All I really wanted was to keep it real. . .'"

Ashley listened in amazement. Wendy had the most awesome voice. But then something even more amazing happened. Tyler grabbed another mike and sang along!

Tyler and Wendy smiled shyly at each other. When the song was over, the Student U went wild.

"Way to go!" Ashley cheered. Clapping, she ran over to Wendy and Tyler.

"I didn't know you liked the Wingnuts!" Tyler told Wendy.

"I didn't know you liked karaoke!" Wendy said.

Ashley grinned and stepped back. Way back. This time she was not going to get in the way.

Tyler handed the controls to another guy. Then he and Wendy walked off to the side.

Ashley sat with the others and watched some more karaoke. But the corner of her eye was glued on Tyler and Wendy. They talked a lot. And laughed a lot. And even sang another duet!

After the party, Tyler helped pack up the equipment. Wendy ran over to Ashley, her face glowing.

"So?" Ashley asked Wendy. "How long did it

take before Tyler asked you out?"

"He didn't," Wendy said.

"Oh," Ashley said, disappointed.

"But we had the most awesome time!" Wendy said, her eyes shining. "And look what he gave me!"

"What?" Ashley asked.

Wendy held up a CD. "It's the Wingnuts' latest CD!" she said. "Tyler just picked it up in town, but he wanted me to have it. Do you believe it?"

"That's a good sign," Ashley pointed out.

"I wish I could give Tyler something," Wendy said. "But I don't have a clue what it should be."

"What kind of stuff does he like?" Ashley asked. "Movies? Books? Electronic games?"

"Giraffes," Wendy said.

"Giraffes?" Ashley wrinkled her nose.

Wendy nodded. "Ever since Tyler was a kid he loved giraffes," she said. "He had giraffe sheets, giraffe wallpaper, giraffe birthday cakes. He even confessed that he still collects stuffed giraffes. Isn't that cute?"

Ashley's eyes widened as she thought of Mr. Stretch. He was a giraffe. He was stuffed, too!

"So what do you think, Ashley?" Wendy asked. "Any ideas for the ideal gift?"

Ashley didn't know what to say. She knew Mr.

CHAPTER THIRTEEN

Stretch would be the perfect gift for Wendy to give to Tyler.

But was she willing to give him up?

"Listen, giraffe!" Mary-Kate told Mr. Stretch. "In just a few minutes Campbell and Phoebe will come into this room. And if they see you and your big feet – I lose the bet!"

Mary-Kate grunted as she lifted Mr. Stretch. It was Thursday afternoon. And Ashley still hadn't ditched the giraffe.

Mary-Kate was totally desperate. There was only one thing left to do. "Come on," Mary-Kate grunted as she lifted Mr. Stretch. "You're going undercover!"

She tried shoving the giraffe under her bed, but his feet stuck out. She tried cramming Mr. Stretch into the wardrobe, but his neck stuck out. She even tried putting a lamp shade over his head – but his tongue hung out!

"Why did you have to be so big?" Mary-Kate complained. "Why couldn't Ashley have picked up a stuffed squirrel?"

Mary-Kate glanced at her watch. If she worked fast enough, she still might be able to hide Mr. Stretch in another room.

"Come on," Mary-Kate said as she lifted the giraffe. She stumbled towards the door. But then she heard footsteps in the hall. And Campbell's and Phoebe's voices!

"Too late," Mary-Kate muttered.

There was a knock, and then the door swung open. Campbell and Phoebe walked into the room. Their eyes lit up when they saw Mr. Stretch.

"Campbell!" Phoebe cried. "Do you see what I see?"

"I sure do," Campbell said. "And you know what that means."

"It means," Phoebe said, "that we—"

"Hi, guys!" Ashley interrupted as she stepped into the room. She looked at Mr. Stretch. "What are you doing with my giraffe?"

"Nothing!" Mary-Kate blurted out. She squeezed Mr. Stretch around his neck. "I just needed a hug!"

"What are you doing here, Ashley?" Phoebe asked. "Aren't you usually at your cider booth around now?"

"Not today." Ashley threw back her shoulders. "I'm here on a mission. You were right about Mr. Stretch, Mary-Kate," she said. "He does take up a lot of room. And as much as I love him, I've decided that it's time to give him away."

Mary-Kate's eyes widened. This was totally unbelievable!

"I knew you'd come around, Ashley," Mary-Kate said, trying to sound as if she really believed it. "So, when are you giving him away?"

"Right now," Ashley said. "Unless you want to hold on to him a little longer."

Was she kidding? "No!" Mary-Kate cried. She tossed the big giraffe at Ashley. "I'm feeling much, much better now!"

Ashley gave Mary-Kate a puzzled look.

"You might want to rethink this, Ashley," Phoebe warned her.

"What if Mr. Stretch winds up in the wrong hands?" Campbell asked. "What if some kid sticks bubble gum all over him?"

"I don't think so." Ashley laughed. "Mr. Stretch is going to be in very good hands."

"Whose hands?" Phoebe asked.

"Who cares?" Mary-Kate said quickly. "As long as Mr. Stretch finds a good home!"

Mary-Kate whisked Ashley and Mr. Stretch out of the room. After closing the door, she turned to Campbell and Phoebe. Mary-Kate didn't know why Ashley had changed her mind, but at this point it didn't really matter.

"Well, you did it, Mary-Kate," Phoebe said. "You aced the ultimate test."

"You got Ashley to give away that goofy giraffe," Campbell said.

CHAPTER FOURTEEN

"Of course I did!" Mary-Kate grinned at her friends. "I said I would, didn't I?"

"Nervous?" Mary-Kate asked.

"Are you kidding?" Ashley said. "If my mouth were any drier, it would be filled with sawdust!"

It was Friday afternoon. In just a few minutes the judging of the apple cider would begin.

This is it, Ashley thought. *This is the day I've been waiting for!*

Crowds of kids were gathering in front of a long table covered with a white tablecloth. On top of the table stood four cups of apple cider.

I wonder which one is mine, Ashley thought.

She spotted Elise in the crowd. Elise gave Ashley a thumbs-up. Then she saw Tyler and Wendy. They were laughing together and eating candyfloss.

Ashley smiled. Her latest strategy was a major success. Just minutes after Wendy gave Mr. Stretch to Tyler, he asked her out. For Saturday night!

Now all I have to do is win this contest, Ashley thought, *and everything will be perfect.*

"I'm sure you're going to win, Ashley," Mary-Kate whispered. "No other cider booth had such a huge turnout."

"I hope you're right," Ashley said. But deep inside she knew she had an excellent chance.

Logan, Ashley thought, *you are about to go down!*

But where was Logan? Ashley scanned the

crowd. She saw the other contestants—Felicia and Owen – but not Logan.

"I wonder where Logan is," Ashley said.

"He probably can't stand the thought of losing," Mary-Kate joked. But then she pointed over Ashley's shoulder. "Wait. Isn't that Logan over there? With Mrs. Pritchard?"

"Where?" Ashley asked. She strained to see where Mary-Kate was pointing. Mrs. Pritchard was walking towards the judging table – with Logan Beecham right behind her.

Logan stared straight at Ashley. He had a sneaky look on his face.

What is he up to? Ashley wondered.

A student adjusted the microphone next to the judging table. Mrs. Pritchard stepped up to the mike and began to speak.

"Students," she said, "I have just been told that the popularity of one of the apple ciders might have been based on a rumour."

Ashley's blood turned to ice. Suddenly she knew what Logan was doing.

"Oh, no, Mary-Kate," Ashley whispered. "Logan is trying to get me disqualified."

"Rumours are unacceptable," Mrs. Pritchard said sternly. "So in order for this contest to be fair, we have planned a little taste test instead."

"A taste test?" Ashley gasped. She caught sight of Elise's face in the crowd. She looked as nervous as Ashley felt.

Everyone watched as a student placed a number in front of each of the four cups.

"Without knowing which apple cider is which," Mrs. Pritchard continued, "we will ask a group of First Formers to judge the best apple cider."

"Your apple cider is awesome," Mary-Kate said. "You still have a great chance!"

Ashley hoped Mary-Kate was right. She watched as five First Formers marched to the table, each carrying a small chalkboard.

As the judges sipped, Ashley wondered which cup was hers – and how much they liked it!

"Thank you, judges," Mrs. Pritchard said when they finished sampling the ciders. "You've tasted each cider recipe. Now please cast your votes."

While the judges scribbled on chalkboards, Ashley grabbed Mary-Kate's hand and gave it a squeeze. When the judges were done, they held up their boards one by one: 3, 2, 3, 3, 3.

Ashley quickly did the maths. "Four votes for cup number three," she said. "But who is number three?"

Excited whispers filled the tent.

"And the winner of this year's apple cider contest is," Mrs. Pritchard announced, "Ashley Burke!"

"It's me! It's me!" Ashley gasped.

"You did it, Ashley!" Mary-Kate cried. "And Logan Beecham didn't even come close!"

"No fair!" Logan started to shout. "I want a recount! A recount!"

The crowd cheered as Mrs. Pritchard pinned a blue ribbon to Ashley's denim jacket. Then Ashley ran back to Mary-Kate and her friends.

"Way to go!" Mary-Kate cheered. She gave Ashley an enormous hug. "I told you your apple cider rules!"

Samantha Kramer tapped Ashley on the shoulder. "If everything was just a rumour," she said slowly, "does this mean your apple cider wasn't a love potion?"

"It wasn't." Ashley sighed. "Sorry, Samantha."

"I'm not!" Samantha said, flashing a huge smile. "That means Philip Jacoby really did like me. Cool!"

Next Jeremy sauntered over. "Hey, cuz," he said. "I knew your apple cider wasn't a love potion."

"You did?" Ashley asked.

"Of course," Jeremy said. "I was always a babe

magnet!"

Ashley rolled her eyes. She and Mary-Kate walked together to the toffee apple stand.

"Tomorrow is Saturday, Ashley," Mary-Kate said. "Let's spend the whole day together and celebrate. We can see a movie in town, go for pizza and ice cream, shop till we drop – just the two of us."

Ashley thought it was a great idea, until she remembered something.

"What's to celebrate?" Ashley sighed. "You're moving out of my room this weekend. And then we'll hardly see each other again."

"True," Mary-Kate agreed. "But we shouldn't have to live together to see each other. From now on let's make more time just to hang out."

Ashley smiled. It was the best idea she had heard in days. "You got it!" She gave her sister a high five. "You and me. Just like old times!"

"Hey, Ashley?" Mary-Kate said. "I'll also let you in on a little secret tomorrow."

"A secret?" Ashley asked.

"Yeah." Mary-Kate sighed. "It's about this crazy bet I had going."

"Okay," Ashley said. "And I'll let you in on a little secret, too."

RECIPE FOR SUCCESS
by Elise Van Hook

What's the recipe for success? Two barrels of apples, fifteen game booths, sixty students ready to have a good time, and a pinch of good weather! This year's Harvest Festival was the best White Oak and Harrington have ever seen. It was a blast and we wanted to take a moment to give you the highlights.

Let's see, which was the best one? Was it when Coach Salvatore accidentally fell into the dunking booth? Or when Brian Maloney got a walnut from Logan's free brownies stuck up his nose? I'm pretty sure most students would say it was horses' lunch with his ice cream cone – and wound up eating some hay!

The biggest highlight of the week for me was when my friend Ashley Burke won the apple cider contest! Since I worked at Ashley's booth, I managed to score her cider recipe to give to all of you. (Don't worry, she said I could!) Here it is:

Take plain old apple cider and pour it into a saucepan. Then sprinkle in some ginger, nutmeg, and cloves. Heat on medium-high for about half an hour, stirring occasionally. Then throw in a whole bunch of cinnamon sticks and cook for another half hour (don't forget to stir!). You'll have yourself some kicked-up apple cider!

That's apple cider, folks. It's NOT a love potion!

GLAM GAB
Totally T-Shirts
by Ashley Burke

Fashion expert Ashley Burke

Tired of your plain old T-shirts? There are tons of ways you can dress up your tees to make them look funky and cool.

• **Go Graffiti!** That's write! Last Saturday we had a Go Graffiti party here at Porter House. It was super-fun – and super-simple! We all wore plain white tees. And we each brought along a permanent marker in our favorite colour. Then we wrote all over our shirts! Here are some things I scribbled on Phoebe Cahill's shirt: BFF! 2 good 2 B 4-gotten! You can write or draw anything you want. And the best part is, penmanship doesn't matter!

• **Cut it up!** Get a little style into your wardrobe with the useful, yet often forgotten glamour tool, scissors! Cut a cute zigzag design to pump up the neckline of that boring tee. Or try cutting vertical strips at the bottom of your shirt. For a burst of colour, slip a bead onto each strip and secure it with a knot at the end!

• **Snip and Sew!** Want to get that "gathered" look on your plain tees? Here's how to do it: take scissors and cut a row of tiny slits (no wider than a quarter) anywhere on your T-shirt. The two most common places for slits are up the middle of the front and up the sleeves, but you can put them anyplace you want. Then using a needle and some ribbon, weave the ribbon through the slits. Pull on the end of the ribbon, and the shirt will instantly look gathered. Just make sure to sew the ends of the ribbon to your shirt so it stays that way!

Take it from me – all three of these options will make your wardrobe tee-rific!

SLIP 'N' SLIDE

Sports pro Mary-Kate Burke

Ooze or Lose!

kick-off this year's Harvest Festival with a Harrington football game (thanks to a giant rainstorm). But I had a lot of fun at the "Ooze-fest" that happened instead!

For everybody who was at "the fest," we're having another one this Saturday. Yeah! For all those who have no idea what an Ooze-fest is, I'll give you a few hints of what it isn't: 1) It's not watching the Harrington guys slip down a muddy field for a touchdown. 2) It has nothing to do with the frog

guts we saw in Biology last week. And 3) It's not – repeat not – about that slime your kid brother always has dripping out his nose!

If you want to know what it is, I suggest you meet the other Oozers in front of the Harrington main building tomorrow at 3:00. See you there!

THE GET-REAL GIRL

Dear Get-Real Girl,

My roommate and I get along great. There's just one problem. She loves to

play the clarinet and practises all the time in our room! I don't mind it once in a while, but all the time is too much! I don't want to be mean, but how can I get her to stop the music?

Signed,
Tuned Out

Dear Tuned,

I hear you (and her – I live down the hall)! Why don't you offer to go over to the music hall with her and listen to her practise every once in a while? That way you'll be showing your support – and she'll get used to going over there to practise!

Signed,
Get-Real Girl

Dear Get-Real Girl,

Two weeks ago my boyfriend dumped me and I've been really sad ever since! I still play "our song" and keep his picture on my desk. I want to move on but I keep thinking that I'll never find anyone I like better. Help!

Signed,
Out of Love

Dear Out of Love,

Step 1: Get Real! There are tons of great guys out there to choose from – and plenty of time to meet them!

Step 2: Get Out There! There's no sense in sitting around moping all the time, especially when you could be out having fun with your friends. Besides, how will you be sure you'll never like anyone better until you meet some new people?

Signed,
Get-Real Girl

THE FIRST FORM BUZZ
by Dana Woletsky

Hanging around the Harvest Festival got me a lot more than some apples and a hayride. I managed to score some great gossip, too!

SS has got it bad for a First Former from Harrington. But I hear he's more interested in listening to his Walkman than listening to her!

Question: aren't we a little old for stuffed animals? I guess AB isn't. Word around Porter House is that she's into stuffed

animals in a BIG way! Speaking of AB, a

Harrington guy with the initials LB tells me that she spread rumours about her apple cider in order to win the contest. Come on, AB. Do you really expect us to believe you invented a love potion?

Then again, love *has* been in the air these days. A certain TK was seen serenading a lucky girl in Porter House the other night. WL wanted the song

to be for her – but it was really for someone else! Remember girls, if you want the scoop, you just gotta snoop!

UPCOMING CALENDAR
Fall/Winter

Clothing shortage alert! No, not in your wardrobe – at the theatre department! They really need some new clothes for their upcoming plays so be sure to get down there and donate some of yours today.

You say you want extra credit? Well, you'll have to do a bit more than clap some dusty erasers. And standing on one foot all term might get you in The Guinness Book of World Records, but it'll do nothing for your grades. So head on down to the program office and sign up for a three-week extra credit class. You'll be glad you did!

Ho! Ho! Holly Helpers is looking for members. Do some good for your fellow classmates and join! The sign-up sheet is posted on the bulletin board outside Mrs. Pritchard's office.

Want to be a pop star? Then stop singing into your hairbrush in front of the mirror. Try singing in

front of an audience instead! Karaoke. Student lounge. Friday night. Be there. Be discovered!

IT'S ALL IN THE STARS
Fall Horoscopes

Leo
(July 22-August 21)

You're always the one eager to make things happen – and you always have a plan to do it! But this month, don't get overexcited about your plans. Make sure to sit down and carefully think about what you're going to do so you don't make any mistakes. That way, when you put your plans into motion, you can sit back and enjoy the ride!

Virgo
(August 22-September 22)

Like the rest of us, deep down, Virgos have their insecurities. But this month, don't let your fears hold you back. Don't be afraid to be the centre of attention, and don't be afraid you won't be able to accomplish your goal. If you put your mind to it, you can do anything!

Libra
(September 23-October 22)

Libras are some of the most ambitious people out there. You're smart and savvy and know how to get places! Just make sure that this month, you don't push yourself too hard. Save your energy for something else. Otherwise, you might burn out before you reach your goal!

"Hmm. This is interesting," Bethany said, pointing to a card. "Somebody is going to give you a present. And it looks like something you really want."

"What is it?" I asked.

"I don't know," she said. "But the cards say you're going to be receiving a present from someone very soon."

I shook my head. "It's not my birthday. And Christmas is two months away. Who would give me a present?" I asked.

Bethany didn't know – that was all she saw.

After I left her, I went back to my dorm. When I arrived, Phoebe and Ginger were hanging out with my roommate, Campbell.

As I flopped down on my bed, Campbell handed me an envelope. "This is for you, Mary-Kate," she said. "It showed up an hour ago. Somebody stuck it under the door."

I took the envelope and opened it. Inside were two tickets to the New Hampshire College women's basketball finals, featuring my favorite team – the Hampshire Hoops!

The game was totally sold out. The tickets were impossible to get. And suddenly I had two of them!

"Incredible!" Campbell exclaimed. "Who sent them?"

I peered in the envelope for a note, but there was nothing else in it except the tickets. I looked at the outside of the envelope. My name was printed on it in block letters. But there was no return address.

That's when I remembered Bethany.

"I can't believe it," I said. "She predicted this would happen!"

"Who?" Phoebe wanted to know.

"Bethany," I told her. "I went back to the carnival today. She read my fortune again and said I'd be getting a gift. And here it is."

"But how could she have known?" Ginger asked.

I stared at the tickets. "I have no idea."

Diary, I never thought I believed in any of this supernatural stuff. But now I'm not so sure . . .

Dear Diary,

My friend, Jill, looked a little worried today, when I finally dragged her to the afternoon performance of the circus. I knew our article about the circus for the school newspaper would be great. I just wished that Jill would relax, so she could take some good pictures.

The clowns were a total hoot. The funniest of them all were a man and a woman who played a married couple. I've never laughed so hard in my life. When their act was over, I clapped until my hands hurt.

"I can't wait to interview them!" I whispered to Jill, after they left the arena.

"Interview them?" Jill said, biting her lower lip. "Oh, I don't know. I mean, do you really want to interview some clowns?"

"Why not?" I asked, getting up to leave. "They were the best part of the show!"

"Yeah," Jill said. "But all the magic disappears when they take off their makeup, you know? It's all about make-believe. It would ruin things to see them without their noses and stuff."

"Then we can talk to them before they take off their makeup," I told her. "Come on. The dressing rooms are right over there!"

That's when Jill grabbed my arm. "Ashley!" she cried. "No way!" And she actually dragged me out of the tent!

Once again, Jill was acting totally strange.

Then, I finally figured it out. Jill must be scared of clowns!

"Look, Jill," I told her. "If you're . . . well . . . nervous around the clowns, I understand. My cousin Jeremy has been scared of clowns ever since he was little. Lots of people are. It's nothing to be ashamed of . . ."

Jill gasped. "Scared of them?"

"Maybe I can help," I offered.

"Believe me, Ashley, you don't understand," she said seriously. "There's absolutely nothing you can do to help."

Diary, what is it with Jill? One minute, she's nice and perfectly okay. Then as soon as we get to the circus, she totally freaks out and seems to have a big secret.

I'm going to find out what she's hiding!

PSST! Take a sneak peek
at

Holiday Magic

③⑧ Holiday Magic

Dear Diary,

Guess what happened, Diary? Even though my friend, Melina, won our dorm's cook-off, everyone at Porter House wants me to make Chunky Chicken Under Cover after all for our holiday restaurant. So now Melina and I are co-chefs.

But I wish I could be happier. Everyone is counting on me to help win the five-star rating. But I still don't know the secret ingredient that makes Mom's pot pie taste great.

Melina isn't happy, either, Diary. I don't know why. I tried to talk to her.

"Working together will make this project even more fun, Melina," I said. "And a lot less work for you."

Melina just nodded. She looked distracted. Or worried.

Or maybe she just doesn't want to talk, I thought. So I kept talking.

"Because you only have to make *one* dessert, Melina. Not a whole bunch," I said. "Do you need help trying to pick one?"

"No, "Melina snapped. "I can do it."

"I don't mean – " There was no point trying to explain. Melina walked out.

What's her problem, Diary? I know Melina is shy, but she's usually not rude. I thought we were friends. Friends are happy for each other. And they help each other out.

But Melina doesn't want my help.

And she isn't happy that we're both chefs.

Some people want to win no matter what. I just didn't think Melina was like that.

But Melina isn't my only problem. I *still* have to figure out the secret ingredient.

I thought I might recognize the secret ingredient if I saw it. Mrs. Bromsky, the dining hall lady, said I could look at her herbs and spices after dinner Sunday night.

Melina was standing by the big stove when I walked into the dining hall kitchen.

"Hi, Melina!" I was glad to see her. I wanted to fix things between us. "I didn't expect to find you here."

"Mrs. Bromsky gave me permission to cook," Melina said.
She stirred something in a pot on the stove. "She'll be back in a few minutes."

"Mrs. Bromsky gave me permission to check the spices," I said. I took a step toward the stove. "What are you making?"

Melina moved so I couldn't look into the pot. "It's just an experiment."

I suspected Melina was guarding a secret recipe. Recipes are a chef's most prized possessions. If Melina didn't want to discuss her recipe, that was okay with me. I changed the subject.

"Maybe you can help me," I said.

Melina was the *perfect* person to ask about the secret ingredient. She had probably learned a lot from her famous chef mother.

"Help with what?" Melina asked.

"One of the seasonings on my mom's recipe is too faded to read," I explained. Everything about the pot pie I baked for the cook-off was the same as my mom's. Except for the taste.

I moved to the racks of spices on the counter. Mrs. Bromsky arranged them in alphabetical order. I read the labels on the jars to myself.

All spice, basil, bay leaves. . .

"The missing seasoning gives the sauce a zesty tang," I told Melina. "Do you have any idea what spice it might be?"

I read more labels to myself. *Celery salt, chives, cinnamon, cloves . . .*

"Different blends of herbs and spices create different aromas and flavors," Melina said.

"Right," I agreed. "That's why I need to know what seasoning I'm missing."

"But there are a zillion possible combinations," Melina said. "So I can't possibly guess."

"Oh." I nodded. "I see your point. Thanks anyway."

Melina's explanation made sense. But I couldn't give up. My mom's pot pie would be a total flop without the secret ingredient.

I kept reading. *Dill, garlic salt, ginger . . .*

"Oh, no!" Melina shrieked and jumped back from the stove.

"What's the matter?" I sprang to help her.

"See what you made me do!" Melina glared at me.

I looked at the pot on the stove. Melina's mysterious mixture was boiling over. Dark brown goo bubbled inside the pot. Globs dribbled down the sides.

"Me?" I was stunned.

"I stopped stirring to talk to you," Melina said. "This is ruined!"

I didn't want to say anything, but I think Melina's recipe was ruined *before* it boiled over. Whatever it was, it smelled awful!

And Melina saw me wrinkle my nose.

"Are you making fun of me, Ashley?" Melina's eyes flashed. She was furious.

"No, Melina!" I couldn't let her think that! "Honest."

"Now I have to clean up this mess." Melina turned the stove off.

"I'm really sorry," I said. "Let me help you – "

"No thanks, Ashley." Melina moved the pan to a cold burner. "I just wanted to be left alone."

I didn't want to make things worse. I left, but I was upset, too.

Melina and I were becoming good friends before the cook-off. Now it looks like our friendship is over because of a silly contest.

Dear Diary,

I helped Rhonda load the rolls into her car. Then I went back to Burger Bistro with her. I sure didn't expect to find Dana Woletsky waiting for us!

"What are you doing here, Dana?" I asked.

"I'm writing a story about the Holiday Dinner for the school newspaper," Dana explained. "Doing something nice for police officers and fire-fighters is a great seasonal topic."

"And we appreciate the publicity, Dana," Rhonda said.

Dana looked at Rhonda. "What's Mary-Kate doing here?"

"She's helping me with the Holiday Dinner," Rhonda said. "It's too bad I can't get more student volunteers. I'm short of help because so many families want to come."

"Just like us," Mary-Kate said. "Porter House has so many reservations some people might have to eat standing up!"

"Our dorm has lots of people coming, too," Dana said. Dana always has to act as if she's better than I am.

"I'm glad we're all doing so well," Rhonda said.

I realized Rhonda didn't want us to argue. Dana took the hint and stopped bickering, too.

"The Holiday Dinner is very important to me," Rhonda went on. "It's a lucky thing Mary-Kate already knows how things work at the Burger Bistro. At least I can count on her. I could use ten more like you, Mary-Kate." Rhonda smiled. "I have to check the phone messages. Be right back."

Dana didn't say anything until Rhonda closed the office door. "So you're waiting on tables at Rhonda's Holiday Dinner? How does everyone at Porter House feel about that?"

"They know I can handle both jobs, Dana," I said. "It's no big deal."

Dana arched an eyebrow. "Gee, I think someone who can be in two places at once is a very big deal."

Huh? I blinked.

"What do you mean?" I asked.

"The Holiday Dinner is *Saturday*." Dana couldn't hide her glee. "The same night the First Form restaurants are open for the White Oak Winter Festival."

I never thought to check the date, Diary! And every time Rhonda and I started talking about the details, something cut the conversation short.

This is a *huge* problem.

I can't back out on Rhonda now. She doesn't have enough help, and I promised.

But I can't let Ashley and everyone else at Porter House down, either.

And I definitely can't be in two places at once.

What am I going to do?

mary-kateandashley

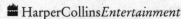

HarperCollins*Entertainment*

PARACHUTE PRESS

DUALSTAR PUBLICATIONS

mary-kateandashley.com
AOL Keyword: mary-kateandashley

TM & © 2002 Dualstar Entertainment Group, LLC.

mary-kateandashley

mary-kateandashley

Sweet 16

(1) *Never Been Kissed*	(0 00 714879 8)
(2) *Wishes and Dreams*	(0 00 714880 1)
(3) *The Perfect Summer*	(0 00 714881 X)

HarperCollins*Entertainment*

PARACHUTE PRESS

DUALSTAR PUBLICATIONS

mary-kateandashley.com
AOL Keyword: mary-kateandashley

MARY-KATE OLSEN ASHLEY OLSEN

BIG FUN IN THE BIG APPLE!

MARY-KATE OLSEN AND ASHLEY OLSEN IN THE BIG SCREEN HIT

Order Form

To order direct from the publishers, just make a list of the titles you want and fill in the form below:

Name ....

Address ....

....

....

Send to: Dept 6, HarperCollins Publishers Ltd, Westerhill Road, Bishopbriggs, Glasgow G64 2QT.

Please enclose a cheque or postal order to the value of the cover price, plus:

UK & BFPO: Add £1.00 for the first book, and 25p per copy for each additional book ordered.

Overseas and Eire: Add £2.95 service charge. Books will be sent by surface mail but quotes for airmail despatch will be given on request.

A 24-hour telephone ordering service is available to holders of Visa, MasterCard, Amex or Switch cards on 0141- 772 2281.

HarperCollins *Children's Books*

mary-kateandashley

TWO of a kind ™

HarperCollins*Entertainment*

 PARACHUTE PRESS

 DUALSTAR PUBLICATIONS

 AOL mary-kate

TM & © 2002 Dualstar Entertainment Group, LLC.

PSST! Take a sneak peek at

37 Hocus Pocus

Dear Diary,

Okay, okay. I know what you're going to say, Diary (that is, if you could talk). Fortune-telling is not for real. It's all just a trick.

Even so, I just couldn't stop thinking about Bethany. Could she really predict the future?

Well, there was only one way I was going to find out.

I hurried over to her trailer at the carnival and went in to talk to her.

"Mary-Kate!" Bethany, the fortune teller, greeted me with a huge smile. "I'm so glad you came back! Sit down."

Bethany took out her Tarot cards and placed five of them down on the table.